Watching the Wheels

Watching the Wheels

Stephen Anthony Brotherton

The Book Guild Ltd

First published in Great Britain in 2023 by
The Book Guild Ltd
Unit E2 Airfield Business Park,
Harrison Road, Market Harborough,
Leicestershire. LE16 7UL
Tel: 0116 2792299
www.bookguild.co.uk
Email: info@bookguild.co.uk
Twitter: @bookguild

Typeset in 12pt Minion Pro

Printed and bound by CPI Group (UK) Ltd, Croydon, CR0 4YY

ISBN 978 1915352 866

British Library Cataloguing in Publication Data.
A catalogue record for this book is available from the British Library.

For Tracey,
who has lived through the creation of every word.
Thank you for your love and patience. xxx

Thank you to Dr Alison Taft
for her supreme guidance and editing skills.

Contents

Home Truths	1
Black Shadow	19
Bug Club	39
Miss Denny's Captain	51
Finding Tommy and Archie	63
Blues and Twos	79
Neighbourhood Watch	94
A Day in the Life of a Head Fairy	104
Mim	115
Roots	125
Invisible Game	136
Coats for Goalposts	149
Locked In	159
Pig	169
Sea Boys	186
Dancing with Dad	204
Guilt Trip	208
A New Beginning	212

Home Truths

6am.

Shitty-fingered Sid stuffed his hand in the cereal box, scooped out a fistful of cornflakes and rammed it into his mouth.

Joe watched him from the lounge and shuddered. Thank God he'd decided to buy his own stuff when he'd moved in. He kept an eye on them as carefully as he could, but he could only do so much. They didn't let you have a fridge, so you had to trust their milk, and all the meals were prepared and served from the main kitchen. The staff were as bad, sneaking off to the sluice to eat stolen bits of dinner out of Matron's gaze, next to the soiled pads and stinking unemptied pots.

Moved in. That implied a choice, but his daughter, Kathy, and the Trotsky social worker had decided. He blamed his son-in-law. He'd heard him grouching about the money. 'That's your inheritance, Kath. And he's giving it away for hand jobs.'

Joe smiled. It'd been worth every penny of the forty quid a throw, plus the twenty quid for the Viagra. 'They're abusing you, Mr Middleton,' said the social worker. Abusing him. It put a bigger smile on his face than the game of bingo they had here every Wednesday. Anyway, it wasn't just a good grip that Sadie gave him. She used to stay and have a cup of tea afterwards, talk about her family, her kids.

'Hey you,' shouted Sid.

Joe sighed. Sid's mind responded to cornflakes by upping its paranoia, like a heroin addict after a hit. There were two certainties in Sid's life, the shit in his fingernails and the knowledge that everyone wanted to harm him. Maybe they did, but there were knives in that drawer. Let the staff risk their lives. It meant waking them up from their armchair doze, but that couldn't be helped.

Joe reached for the buzzer.

*

Nellie opened her one eye. 'If that's Joe again,' she said, 'I'm tying that buzzer out of his reach.'

'I'll go,' said Barbara, pushing away the lounge chair she'd had her feet on and slipping on her shoes.

'He's a pain in the arse,' said Nellie. 'He's only been here two weeks and I'm already sick of him.'

'I think he's frightened of Sid,' said Barbara.

'He needs tying up as well,' said Nellie. 'I told Matron not to stop his sleeping pills.'

Barbara slouched out of the lounge. Nellie rolled on her side and looked at her watch. Nearly time to start getting them up anyway. Fifty-two residents before the morning shift came on duty. A big ask, but the rules had to be followed. Night staff get them up; morning staff do the baths; evening staff put them to bed. Any exceptions got a red ink note in the report book from Matron, and Nellie hadn't had one of those in her forty years of working here. Forty years. She'd have to think about retiring soon. Not yet, though. She still had some life in her. She sat up, stretched and groaned as her muscles and bones objected to the movement. A cup of milky coffee first. That Joe needed a lesson. She'd have to do it out of Barbara's sight. The world had become too soft now; everyone wanted you to mollycoddle them. Not like when she ruled the shift with her sister, May, but those days were gone.

Nellie pushed the chair away, slipped on her shoes, stood up and walked over to the door-length windows that covered the far wall. She pushed back the heavy velvet curtains and, hands on hips, surveyed her Black Country in all its grime and glory. A murky, misty sky. It seemed to take longer to get light now, as though the sun had given up its struggle to break through. She thought of Ted, her husband, his promise of travelling the world, the reality of them rarely venturing over the border in their forty-five years together. Ted in name and in music back then, a greased-back D.A. rock and roller, wooing her with Elvis Presley's "I Got Stung" and "Stuck on You". This morphed into a life of beer, horse racing, cigarettes and giving her a backhander if his tea wasn't on the table at 6pm sharp, ready for the news. Most of the staff were the same. She knew what their lives were like. There were no secrets.

She turned back to the chair that had been her sleeping pitch for the last couple of hours, picked up the empty mugs and walked off towards the kitchen to light the gas stove and boil some milk.

*

Floss stared at her bedroom ceiling. She'd heard the new bloke in the room next door get up and go down to the lounge. Joe. An early riser. She liked that. It showed energy and hope, and he had twinkling blue-grey eyes. He'd sat by her one afternoon and they'd watched a Jimmy Cagney film, *Angels with Dirty Faces*. That witch of a care assistant, Nellie, had taken the mickey, 'Oh, Floss has got a boyfriend.'

Floss had expected Joe to move chairs out of embarrassment, but he'd taken Floss's hand and squeezed it. 'Ignore her,' he'd whispered, and they'd carried on watching the film. His hand felt good, warm, soothing. 'Good film that,' he'd said at the end. 'One of his best.'

It was. Floss had seen it during the war at the Walsall Odeon with her American officer. Lieutenant Vance Gallagher. He had blue eyes as well, but his were wrinkle free and more of an azure lagoon shade.

Vance. She hadn't thought about him for years. They used to make love in a bluebell wood in the middle of Cannock Chase, birdsong in her ears, blue sky through the tree canopy, her wearing the silk stockings he'd bought, him gasping when he'd found the bare thigh flesh underneath her suspenders. She could still hear that gasp. 'I'll dream of your thighs before I go into battle,' he'd said. 'It'll make charging those Nazis a piece of cake.'

She touched her left thigh underneath the bedclothes, her hand landing on the tip of a damp continence pad, which had slipped out of her netty pants. At least she had her mind, and her memories. She'd caught her refection the other day in the dressing table mirror. They'd given her a cup of tea whilst she was on the commode. She looked like a dead bird. It could be worse. She could be that Esther woman who sang everything in a robotic voice, *I'm eating my peas now… I'm going to the toilet now.* Floss squeezed her eyes together. No more tears.

Vance. He'd survived the war, gone back home to grow potatoes in Idaho. He wrote to her for a few years, promising to visit when he was sorted, but that had tailed off. Their moment had passed. She wondered what sort of life he'd had, whether he'd ever thought about the woods and her thighs, whether he'd gasped time and time again with another woman. She hoped so.

*

Barbara sat in Joe's bedroom chair. He watched her carefully. She took the hem of her uniform dress and hitched it up her thighs, just enough so he could see the start of bare flesh at the top of her stockings. She saw the flush come into his face. 'Are you okay?' she said.

'Very,' said Joe. 'Can you go a little higher?'

She shuffled back and more of her thigh and suspenders came into view. 'I hope you appreciate this, Joe,' she said. 'It's not easy working in these things.'

'I do,' he said. 'I think I can feel some life coming back.'

'None of that,' she said, standing up. 'I don't mind giving you a flash, but I'm not doing anything else.' She walked over to the bed.

'Thank you,' he said as she sat down beside him.

She kissed him on the forehead, realising he'd take a sneaky look down the top of her dress.

'You're wearing that red bra again,' he said.

'And you shouldn't be looking,' she said. 'Now, let me get you that cup of tea. And leave the buzzer alone. Nellie's not happy.'

'Dried up old prune,' he said. 'You know what she needs.'

'That may be so,' said Barbara, 'but you need to be careful.'

She walked out of the bedroom towards the kitchen, smiling to herself. She wondered what her career-long civil servant husband and her two married daughters would think. Stockings, suspenders, making an old man's cheeks burst with excitement. It did no harm. She'd heard about the prostitutes. Good for Joe. At least his money hadn't been wasted. She might pop down to the cap and scarf cupboard later and get him a nice set. A legacy of all the old men that had died here. The family never wanted their clothes.

The suspender belt rustled against her dress as she bustled down the corridor. She needed to go and put her tights back on before the early morning rush started.

*

Joe patted the rhino skin lump in his groin. He thought about the young lad who'd started work experience this week, how he'd recoiled in horror when he'd seen Joe's hernia. 'It's not catching, is it?' the lad had said. Joe hadn't seen him since, which wasn't surprising. Letting young boys see things like that. They should be ashamed of themselves.

Joe pulled up his trousers. He'd been trying to get some life going, but he needed the Viagra, at least that's what his head told him. Still, a flash from Barbara would do for now. She'd been a bit red-cheeked when she'd left, a bit overexcited. Naïve, but caring. He'd never tell anyone. He hoped she knew that. He laughed and wondered what his daughter and the Trotsky would make of it.

Nellie. He'd noticed the cruel look in her eyes, and he'd seen her with the teapots – brown pot, no sugar; stainless steel pot, sugar. They usually ran out on the last bit of their early morning trolley trip, which meant going back to the kitchen for more hot water. Not Nellie. She always topped it up in the sluice.

He lay back down on the bed. He liked that old woman, Floss. She didn't say much, but that suited him fine, and she liked Jimmy Cagney films. He thought about his wife, Betty. She never had any patience with stockings and suspenders, or hand jobs. 'Lovemaking, Joe,' she used to say. 'That's what we do. None of this sex business.' For over fifty years she'd been right, and then she'd gone, massive stoke. She hadn't suffered. Never woke up, dead in a week. There were worse ways to check out, but he'd like to have said goodbye. He remembered the first time he saw Betty, on Cleethorpes pier, the wind blowing hard, her trying to keep her dress from blowing over her head. He'd taken a deep breath and asked if she wanted to go indoors, get a coffee and a piece of cake. To his surprise she'd said yes. Best two shillings he'd ever spent. She'd made him wait a month before he kissed her, but he could still remember the taste of her lips.

He pushed the thought away. Nearly time for breakfast.

He hoped Sid had been locked up somewhere safe.

*

Two days later, Barbara found herself on a morning shift. A bit of overtime to help buy her grandson, Tim, a remote-controlled car. She had her stockings on again, but Joe seemed distracted. 'Are you feeling okay?' she said.

'I feel a bit off to be honest,' said Joe. 'Perhaps I'm coming down with something.'

She put her hand on his forehead. He felt fine. She'd noticed he hadn't peeked down the top of her dress, even though she'd left an extra button open. Perhaps he'd gone off her.

'It's not you,' he said.

'No. But I suppose looking at my thighs from a distance does have a shelf life.'

'They're very nice thighs,' said Joe, smiling.

'But you want more. I can't do that, Joe. It's only meant to be a bit of fun, to cheer you up.'

'And it did. It cheered me up a lot.'

'You're a sweet man,' she said, touching his cheek.

Joe frowned. 'I'm an old man,' he said, reaching over and picking up a folded piece of ripped in half notepaper from the dressing table.

He handed it to Barbara.

'What's this?' she said.

'A telephone number,' he said. 'I don't have many days left.'

Barbara unfolded the paper. 'Who's Sadie?'

Joe smiled. 'A friend. A very good friend.'

Barbara closed the bedroom door behind her. She felt disappointed. 'Stop being ridiculous,' she told herself.

'He's an old man who you gave a little thrill. That's all.' She sighed. The way he'd looked at her when he'd seen her stockings, the expectation when she'd hitched up her dress. Her stomach tightened at the thought. But now he wanted more. She opened up the paper he'd given her. A phone call. That's all it would take.

She forced herself to think about something else. Her daughter, Amy. Twenty-six years of age, running back home every time her husband, Rob, blew his nose the wrong way. 'Bring me a cup of hot chocolate, Mum,' she'd said when she came through the door last night. 'I'm going up to bed.' That would be it for a week now. Mum, do this. Mum, do that. Still, she'd go again soon, until the next time.

*

Nellie folded up the ironing and placed it in the room baskets, ready to be distributed around the home on a trolley. Some of the names on the clothes, especially the underwear, had faded, so she guessed who owned what. She didn't worry too much. It had all been washed.

She winced and put her hand on her ribs. Ted had been in a foul mood last night. She hoped his horses had won today. She blinked, took off her tinted glasses and wiped them on her sleeve. She put her hand in her overall pocket, pulled out a paper tissue and dabbed her eyes. Damn cataracts. She should have heard about the operation by now. She put the glasses back on her face.

Barbara opened the laundry door.

Where've you been?' said Nellie.

'Just popped in to see Joe,' said Barbara. 'Making sure Sid wasn't upsetting him.'

'He's got to learn to stand on his own two feet,' said Nellie, folding up a pair of corduroy trousers and placing them in a basket. 'Anyway, he's got his friend, Floss, to cheer him up.'

Barbara nodded and pushed the trolley out of the laundry.

Nellie watched her go. Joe. All that popping down to see him for no reason. She knew what was going on. She'd seen it before, a long time ago. One of the night staff, down on her luck, rubbish marriage, in need of extra cash. The oldest trade in the world.

And Nellie could see the suspenders through Barbara's thin cotton dress.

*

Floss glared at the new man, Mike. A blond-haired cockney who'd only been in the home a few hours. He grinned at her and then spat in the lavender potpourri that the cleaner, Joyce, had put on the coffee table to brighten up the lounge. 'That's potted that pourri, mate,' he said to Joe, who had just finished making himself and Floss a cup of tea in the kitchenette.

Joe ignored him, walked back into the lounge and sat down next to Floss. He put the two cups of tea on the coffee table, took Floss's hand in his and leaned towards her. 'Have you had a good day?' he said.

Floss smiled at him. She wished she could talk to him properly, but the stroke had robbed that from her. Odd words she could manage, but not without dribbling, and she didn't want to dribble in front of Joe. If only he could hear the thoughts in her head. She felt herself blush. For a start, she'd tell him he had a wonderful smile.

'What have you been doing today?' said Joe, still holding her hand. 'I can see you've had your hair done. It looks lovely.'

'Had her hair done,' said Mike. 'I shouldn't think it ever looks any bloody different.'

Floss saw the smile disappear from Joe's face. He let go of her hand. 'Excuse me a second,' he said, standing up and walking back across the lounge. He put his hand across Mike's throat, dragged him out of his chair and across the carpet. 'Apologise,' he said.

Mike fell on his knees in front of Floss. 'You're choking me,' he spluttered.

'Apologise,' said Joe, tightening his grip.

'Joe,' shouted Barbara, coming into the lounge pushing the laundry trolley. 'What on Earth…'

'Apologise,' said Joe again.

'I'm sorry,' Mike spluttered. 'I'm sorry.'

Joe let go of him and sat back down next to Floss. He took her hand again.

Barbara ran over to Mike. 'Are you okay?' she said, kneeling down beside him.

'He's okay,' said Joe. 'He just needs to learn some manners.'

Floss squeezed Joe's hand.

*

Joe pulled the plug out of the washbasin, picked up the hand towel and wiped the shaving suds from his face. Betty liked him to shave twice a day, and he couldn't break the habit. 'I like you clean and smooth,' she used to say, rubbing his cheeks. 'Now go and put some of that tangy aftershave on I bought you.' Old Spice. He wondered if you could still get it. He looked around the bedroom for his shirt.

'Visitor for you,' said Nellie, knocking once and opening the door. 'It's your niece.'

'Thank you,' said Joe.

Nellie stood in the doorway. 'You've been before?' she said to the woman.

'No. I've only just found out the address.'

'Okay. But don't stay too long. It's nearly lunchtime.'

Nellie closed the bedroom door.

Joe heard her walk away up the corridor. 'Sadie,' he said.

'Uncle Joe. It looks like I've caught you in your vest.'

*

Barbara finished setting the tables for lunch, waiting for Nellie to come back to the lounge. She looked across at Mike. He'd been very sheepish since the incident earlier. Floss still looked pleased with herself. Barbara hoped Joe would carry on looking after her. She liked Floss.

'Well,' said Nellie, walking out of the bedroom corridor. 'There's something not right there.'

'Where?' said Barbara. 'Has Sid woken up?'

'Joe's niece,' said Nellie. 'The way they're looking at each other.'

'What way?'

'You know. The way people look when they've been, you know…'

'With his niece…'

'That's the point. I don't think she is his niece. You know what happened when he was at home.'

'You don't think…' said Barbara.

'Why not? It's happened here before.'

'Joe wouldn't… not here. He wouldn't be that brazen.'

'He would, and I think you know he would.'

'What do you mean?' said Barbara. 'And what do you mean by the way they look at each other? You're imagining it.'

Nellie reached over, pinched the fabric of Barbara's uniform dress together and twanged one of the suspender straps. 'Like I'm imagining these.'

Barbara stepped back, her face pumped with blood. 'It's none of your business what I wear.'

'It is when it interferes with your work. How much is he paying you?'

'It's not like that,' said Barbara.

'Really,' said Nellie. 'I didn't wash up with the tide, you know. I hope you get him to cover it up. Looks like you're on a list.'

*

Floss kept her eye on Nellie and Barbara, waiting for the right moment to try and get their attention. She wanted to go to the toilet and back before everyone else took their seats. She didn't want to run the risk of Joe not sitting by her. She glanced at the clock. Five minutes to one. Joe would be back in a minute. Punctual. Like her American lieutenant. 'A man should always be on time,' he used to say, in his Idahoan drawl. 'A woman. Well, that's different. It's your prerogative to be a little late.' She smiled at the memory. That Mike wouldn't bother her again, not after Joe had come to her rescue.

Nellie walked towards her. 'Come on, Floss,' she said. 'Let's get you toileted before lunch.'

Floss winced. Thank God Joe hadn't heard that.

She felt Nellie's touch on her arm, urging her to move.

Floss put her hand on her tripod, rocked herself against the vinyl chair and stood up.

'That's right,' said Nellie. 'You want to look your best for your fancy man, don't you?'

Floss winced again.

*

Nellie placed the last of blind Henry's scarves on the laundry shelf. He'd died last Thursday, only lingering for a couple of nights, which suited his family but left Nellie feeling short-changed. She preferred it to go on for weeks, forced familial banter, decades-old feuds dug up and given another ten rounds, siblings emotionally blackmailing each other with who gets what ultimatums. Everyone watching, waiting for the last breath, no one daring to leave the bedside. She'd seen them fighting in the garden before now, two brothers knocking lumps out of each other, arguing about who got the best Christmas present when they were ten, which, somehow, to them, proved Dad had loved one of them more.

Henry had spared everyone by shuffling off quickly.

Nellie had been on nights when he'd gone. She'd checked him at 3am, felt for a pulse, conscious of the family leaning forward to hear the verdict. She'd wanted to lie, keep them waiting, but everyone seemed so fussy about that sort of thing nowadays.

She looked at her watch. 2.30pm. The end of her shift. She'd agreed to meet Barbara in the garden before they went home. She'd expected it. An apology, a clear the air chat. She fastened up her anorak, walked down the corridor, turned off the alarm above the fire door and went outside. She sucked in the crisp autumnal air. Her favourite season, despite the deteriorating light. She liked the trees and plants bare, especially the red dogwood. As she turned the corner by the big oak tree, she saw Barbara waiting for her, sitting on one of the metal benches, next to the rose bushes. She reached the bench. Barbara patted the seat. Nellie sat down. 'You don't have to say anything,' said Nellie. 'We're still friends. We just need to sort out this Joe and everything can go back to normal.'

Barbara slapped her across the cheek.

Nellie gasped, reached up and held her face. She felt tears welling in her eyes. 'What the–'

'This all stops now,' said Barbara, grabbing Nellie's coat by the collar and pulling her face to face. 'You're going to retire.'

Nellie tried to push her away, but Barbara gripped her tight. 'You're old, Nellie,' she said. 'Your days of ruling the roost are over.'

'What do you mean?' Nellie spluttered, cursing the tears that she felt rolling out from underneath her tinted glasses. She wanted to get up, walk away, but Barbara's grip kept her pinned to the bench.

'I mean you and your evil sister aren't in charge anymore.'

'And you are?' said Nellie. 'Matron won't stand for that.'

'I'm not going to Matron. I'm going to the police.'

'The police?'

'All those years of evidence,' said Barbara. 'I think we could get enough of the staff to talk.'

'They'd laugh at you,' said Nellie. 'No one's going to join in with anything like that. And all the residents are long dead.'

'Maybe,' said Barbara. 'But the world's changed. They might just be interested now. People are going to jail for less. Is that something you're prepared to risk?'

Nellie freed herself and stood up. 'You can do what you want. Maybe I'll do some reporting of my own, about you and your kinky underwear.'

'Perhaps you're right,' said Barbara. 'Anyway, I don't need the police.'

'What are you talking about?' said Nellie.

Barbara stood up and grabbed Nellie's coat again. 'I'm talking about you. Blind, old, arthritic you. Maybe I'll just stay here and slap you every time you bully one of them.'

Nellie felt spittle land on her nose. She touched her cheek again. She could see Ted's face in her head, yelling at her because tea wasn't ready. And now this. 'What do you want?' she said.

'I want you to leave Joe alone.'

'Is that it?'

'For now,' said Barbara. 'But you're going to change. I mean it.'

Nellie nodded. 'I want to go home,' she said.

Barbara let go of her coat.

*

Two wall lights lit up the lounge.

The night staff had switched off the big light to try and encourage everyone to bed – like closing time at the pub, said Joe. He and Floss were watching Minder. Everyone else had gone to their room. Joe said Arthur Daley reminded him of his dad, a cockney wide boy chancer. He didn't mind the wall lights, neither did Floss. It made the room cosier, more like home. They were holding hands.

Floss felt him stroking her wedding ring. She wondered how that made him feel. 'Your husband was a lucky man,' he said.

She nodded, wished she could answer him, but the dribbling would start and that wouldn't do. She'd tell him how Dan, her husband, had worked hard, been a family man with rough hands and kind eyes. Not an American Lieutenant, but good enough.

'My Betty had to put up with me for over fifty years,' said Joe. 'I punched well above my weight there.'

Floss saw the tears in his eyes. He looked as though he'd drifted off to another time, another place. This age, this home, these staff. Neither of them belonged here, but they needed to make the most of it.

She squeezed his hand.

'This is nice,' he said, returning her squeeze. 'Shall we watch the news?'

'You're a good soul,' she said, putting a tissue up to her mouth.

Joe leaned down, lowered the tissue and kissed her lips. 'So are you,' he said. 'So are you.'

Black Shadow

I placed a furry cat's head bookmark into my Faber and Faber collector's edition of Charles Dickens' *Great Expectations*, closed the book, placed it on the oak card table in front of me and surveyed the car park through the French doors. I thought for a moment a bleary mist had descended but realised I still had my reading glasses perched on the end of my nose. 'Bloody old fool,' I said, removing my spectacles and easing back in the red leather armchair.

Six weeks had flown by. They told me over a hundred people crammed into this communal lounge for the Christmas party, Harvest festival, Easter bonnet parade, but for the rest of the year it remained cold, echoey and empty. A place of solitude. A perfect retreat inside the care home to layer up, read Dickens and watch the world go by.

On my first Saturday they'd held a jumble sale, the local populace queuing up from 6am in their jogging bottoms, kids hanging from every limb, the crush to get in knocking Matron sideways when she opened the doors. I'd intervened when a bloke wearing a string vest had tried to barter with one of the younger care assistants, Louise, over a 10p pair of socks. 'I'll give you 2p for them,' said the vest bloke.

'Look, mate,' I said. 'They're trying to raise a bit of money for the comforts fund here. There's no discount on 10p.' The bloke threw the socks on the floor and walked off. Louise smiled at me and mouthed, thank you.

Bath time helped me get the staff onside, my flaccid penis flopping forwards, breaking up the foamy water like an icebreaker. I thanked Dad for the gene. Even one of the cooks came to have a look, blurting out a lame excuse of bringing clean towels. I found out later they kept a chart in the staffroom, awarding points for length and girth. Mine had shot off the scale. And then I'd got one of my testicles trapped in the bath chair. That needed an audience to set me free. It didn't hurt; everyone laughed. One of the care assistants, Barbara, a kind soul, a talker who knew when to leave you in peace, freed it with a teaspoon. Her mate, Sheila, put her finger in her mouth and made a popping noise when it came out. 'Jesus, Fred,' said Barbara. 'You'll have to keep your hands on that Percy. You'll have me eye out when I'm trying to find the soap.'

The lounge door opened.

'You okay there, Fred?' said Barbara, poking her head into the room. 'Do you fancy a cup of tea?'

'Lovely,' I said. 'Any chance of a Jammie Dodger?'

'Coming right up,' said Barbara, closing the door.

I watched through the nets covering the floor-to-ceiling corridor windows. Barbara left the tea trolley and walked off towards the kitchen, probably to fetch my biscuits. Nellie, the fierce one with tinted glasses, wouldn't have even offered me a drink in here. 'You need to come to the kitchen,' she'd said last week. 'It's not my job to chase you all over the bloody home.'

I hadn't made a fuss. I didn't mind missing the odd cup of tea if it meant this haven of peace and quiet. I liked a chat, but not that often. It came from a life of getting lost in my head for hours.

The lounge door opened again.

Rhoda raced in, her walking stick barely touching the floor as she sped across the carpet towards me.

*

I first came across Rhoda at tea on my second day in the home. We were all in the dining room and I heard raised voices coming from the table in front of the serving counter. The next thing I knew, two women had struggled to their feet, picked up their walking sticks and clashed them together in sword-fighting mode. One of the women, Rhoda, shouted, 'I'm going to beat you to death, you old witch.' With that, she scooped her weapon low and rattled her opponent's ankles. The other woman, Gwen, screamed and went down on her knees. Rhoda lifted her stick in the air, but it was grabbed from behind by Matron. 'Let go of me,' said Rhoda, her auburn wig sliding backwards across her scalp.

'Give it to me, Rhoda,' said Matron.

The wig gave way to gravity and fell to the floor. Rhoda let go of her stick and put her two hands on her head, wisps of grey hair poking through her fingers. She burst into uncontrollable laughter. I joined in, as did most of the dining room.

Barbara helped a limping Gwen out of the lounge.

'That's more than enough entertainment for one day,'

said Matron. 'Come with me, Rhoda. I need to fill out another one of those reports.'

Rhoda held her coffee mug in the air, like the winning captain holding up the FA cup. 'A hattrick this week,' she said. 'Is that some kind of a record?'

Matron smiled and shook her head.

I clapped, which made everyone turn and look at me.

'Rhoda pinched Gwen's boiled egg,' Barbara told me later. 'Said she paid more money than her and should get more of the rations. Gwen threw salt at her, and they started stick fighting.'

'She's got spirit,' I said.

'You stay away,' said Barbara. 'She's trouble that one.'

The next morning, I sat by Rhoda at breakfast. 'They've told me to stay away from you,' I said.

'Sounds like good advice,' said Rhoda, pouring milk over her sugar puffs.

*

Rhoda made it across the sticky communal lounge carpet and sat down in the armchair next to me. 'Alright?' she said, straightening her wig.

'I am,' I said.

'I've told that Barbara I'm joining you for tea. Did she say yes to the biscuits?'

'Jammie Dodgers. As you requested.'

'Good lad,' she said, patting my knee. 'That member of yours works every time.'

Barbara opened the door and wheeled a trolley towards us. 'Here they are,' she said. 'Batman and Robin.'

'We'd prefer the Lone Ranger and Tonto,' said Rhoda.

'Or maybe Laurel and Hardy,' I said.

'You can be the fat one,' said Rhoda.

Barbara put two mugs of tea and a plate of biscuits on the table. 'Don't let Nellie see these,' she said, before pushing her trolley away and walking out of the lounge.

'Nellie,' said Rhoda, dunking a Jammie Dodger in her tea, 'wouldn't have lasted five minutes in Kenya.'

'How long were you there?' I said.

'Nearly twenty years. My husband, Billy, owned a coffee plantation.'

'What made you come back?'

'They fell out with honkies. And neither of us wanted to get skinned.'

'You must have made your money though. Owning a coffee plantation.'

Rhoda crunched her biscuit, the top and bottom set of her ill-fitting false teeth moving independently of each other. She'd smothered her lips in double-decker red lipstick, gunges of which had stuck to her incisors. I noticed her wig had slipped again, this time over her left ear. 'Kenya is the only place you can spend money made in Kenya,' she said. 'That's why I'm stuck in this dog hole. Thank God Billy's dead. Did I tell you about my Billy? A wine waiter sort of man. You'd have liked him.'

'He sounds fun,' I said.

'Oh, he was. We met in the casino, playing the roulette wheel. Pissed as farts we were. Slept it off on the nudist beach. Burned the cheeks of his arse and the soles of his feet. Couldn't sit down or walk for a week. And then there was Monte Carlo. Billy's mate lent him his Chevy Corvette and we drove along the strip, my hair blowing all over the place. He said I was his Ali MacGraw and he was my Steve McQueen. We met Audie Murphy once in Venice, surprisingly short for a war hero. And then there was the time…'

I held the coffee mug to my face, listened and thought about my life. Broseley kid, married my first girlfriend, Jessie, never been abroad, barely been out of Shropshire. We stayed in a caravan in Cornwall once but drove home early because it rained. Window cleaner, chamois leather, proper ladders, never fell off once, timing my lunchbreaks to sit on the hilltop house roof, eating my cheese and onion sandwiches, sucking in the views of the Wrekin. Fifty years later, Jessie died, and I moved in here.

Only one chapter left.

'Are you okay?' said Rhoda. 'You seem miles away.'

I put the coffee mug on the table. 'Just thinking,' I said. 'Your stories make me feel like I've never lived.'

'Well,' she said. 'It wasn't all tits and tinsel. I miss out the rubbish bits, all the years after Billy died when I tried to drink myself into oblivion with vodkas and tonics, when I smelt worse than my cats, when Blockbusters was the highlight of my day.'

'But at least you had the good bits. The only story I have is my dad's inheritance.'

Rhoda nodded at my groin. 'It's a pretty good tale if you ask me.'

'Wish I'd lived a bit more,' I said.

She patted my leg again. 'You had a wonderful wife.'

'I know. But I've missed out on excitement. Always too afraid, I guess.'

'Well, you're not dead yet.'

'I might as well be with this body.'

'Rubbish. What would you like to do?'

'It's too late.'

'What would make you happy?' she said.

'Grandad let me drive his steamroller once.'

'A steamroller? A bloody steamroller?'

'It's all I can think of. I never did anything. Our kid let me watch him speedway race at Perry Barr, but he wouldn't let me near his bike. We could go and watch that I suppose.'

'Leave it with me,' said Rhoda, picking up another biscuit. 'I might have an idea.'

*

The following evening my daughter, Jody, visited. We sat in the dining room. Jody said she couldn't stand the cold in the communal lounge. 'It's like one of those Dickens' workhouses,' she said. 'I'm sure that's why you love it.'

Barbara brought us a tray of tea.

'Has he been behaving himself?' Jody asked her.

'He's lovely,' said Barbara. 'Aren't you, Fred?'

'Always,' I said.

Barbara smiled. 'You have your moments, though,' she said. 'I'm off for my break now. Ring the buzzer if you need anything.'

'What did she mean?' said Jody, crinkling her eyes at me. 'Your moments.'

'No idea. Just something to say I expect.'

'Has something happened, Dad? You look different.'

'Such as?' I said, reaching over and pouring us both a cup of tea.

'I'm not sure, but something's changed.'

I wanted to tell her about Rhoda, but I felt a buzz from having a secret, something of my own. These child-parent visits made me feel like a kid at boarding school, giving a weekly update report, justifying the fees. It's strange, that point in your life when you realise roles have reversed. Your kids are asking and saying the things you used to say to them. Put your coat on. It's cold out. Are you getting enough to eat? Have you made any friends? And they expect a full response. Anything regarded as incomplete is viewed with suspicion, like you're up to something you shouldn't be. Answer the question. Answer the question.

'So who's Rhoda then?' said Jody, taking a sip of her tea.

'Rhoda?' I said.

'Matron told me you've been chatting to someone called Rhoda.'

'Oh,' I said. 'Just someone I've sat next to at dinner a couple of times.'

'Really. Matron says she joins you in your Dickens' room for coffee. It's okay, Dad. I'm pleased you've got a friend.'

'She's an acquaintance. Nothing more.'

'Now don't go all sulky. I'm just saying it's okay with me.'

'Didn't know I needed your permission. And that Matron's got no right telling you my personal business.'

'Dad. I didn't mean anything.'

'Well,' I said. 'It's private. I can still have a private life, can I?'

'Yes,' she said. 'Of course you can.'

I felt the guilt wash over me. She looked shocked, like I'd slapped her. 'I'm sorry for snapping,' I said.

*

'Good for you,' Rhoda said when I told her. 'My kids are the same. Think they have a right to know everything about me. I tell them to bugger off or, better still, ask them questions they don't want to answer, like how many times a week they have sex.'

'That's not me though,' I said. 'I'm Mr Dull.'

'And I suppose I'm your guilty secret. I can't imagine you've had too many people like me in your life.'

'No. Not really. Sorry.'

'Oh, don't apologise. I like it. Perhaps I should meet them and wow them with my tilting wig.'

'Perhaps not,' I said. 'I just…'

'Want something of your own,' she said.

I nodded.

'We're only friends, you know.'

'I know. I know.'

'Anyway, I might have sorted this adventure of yours.'

'What do you mean?'

'I mean,' she said. 'I've booked you a motorbike ride.'

*

Late evening, subdued lighting, curtains closed, everything locked down, the two night staff encouraging slumber with hot, milky drinks and tranquillisers, marching the reluctant ones to their bedrooms.

Rhoda sat by my side on a blue vinyl, two-seater settee in our communal lounge sanctuary, both of us sliding low in the seats, our backs to the corridor windows, our heads together, conspiratorial style, out of view. 'We need to leave early morning,' she whispered. 'About six-thirty.'

'Why so early?' I said.

'Because the Gestapo will be busy getting everyone up.'

'The front door will be locked.'

'No problem,' she said. 'We'll go out the fire door at the bottom of the corridor. I've got a key for the alarm.'

'You've… how did you manage that?'

'They leave it in there all day. I lifted it about a week ago. They signed it off as lost.'

I kissed her on the forehead, her wig slipped forwards. 'You're a marvel,' I said.

'It's easy,' she said, straightening her wig. 'One of the advantages of getting old is everyone thinks you're incapable, and that means you can get away with murder. My grandson, Barney, will be waiting in the car park.'

'It's real,' I said.

'Tomorrow you're going to ride a motorbike,' she said, patting my leg.

'You know I've never ridden a bike.'

'Don't worry. Barney will take you round.'

'What about the track? Has he got that sorted?'

'His mate's got a farm. They use it all the time. You just need to cling on for dear life. If you survive, I'll have a go.'

'You'll have to take that off,' I said, nodding at her wig. 'I don't fancy climbing a tree to retrieve it. Do we need to synchronise our watches?'

'What a good idea,' said Rhoda.

The lounge door opened.

'It's time you two were in bed,' said Nellie.

'What a thing to suggest,' said Rhoda, turning and popping her head above the back of the settee. 'I'm a lady, and we're just good friends.'

*

The pigeons woo, woo, wooed their dawn chorus.

I got dressed, long johns, a couple of vests, a lumberjack shirt, Arran wool jumper, thick cord trousers, Berghaus walking boots. I lay on the bed waiting for Rhoda's three knocks. Everything she said and did seemed to come straight out of a John le Carré book. I half expected a piece of paper to be slipped under my door saying, "Let's rendezvous in Prague".

Tap. Tap. Tap.

I pulled on my suede flying jacket, rammed a grandad cap on my head and opened the door.

'You ready,' she said, smiling at me, smudges of red lipstick on her false teeth. She'd dressed for the cold, a camouflage green Parka coat with a furry hood, thick black tights, red pixie boots and a purple pom-pom hat, which was pinning down her wig.

'As I'll ever be,' I said, pulling on my gloves and closing the door behind me.

'Are you excited?' she said, grabbing my hand.

'Like a schoolboy,' I said. 'I'm a bit nervous as well.'

'Good job you've got me then,' she said.

We walked down the corridor, Rhoda leaning on her stick, me leaning on mine. I had to put my stick in my left hand to hold hands with her. When we arrived at the fire door, she reached into the pocket of her Parka, fetched out the key and placed it in my hand. 'Turn it off then, longshanks,' she said, gesturing towards the alarm's isolation switch above the door.

I did as she asked.

We opened the door, held hands again and stepped outside to face the deserted car park. The ice air made us gasp. The light from the fire door lit up the ground in front of us; glistening spores of frost covered the tarmac path. 'We need to be careful here,' I said, squeezing her hand.

Rhoda nodded and we gingerly stepped forward.

'There he is,' said Rhoda, pointing to the car park.

A black Range Rover with tinted windows flashed its lights.

'Jesus,' I said. 'It really is like a spy story.'

Barney got out of the car and ambled over to us. American white teeth, a gold stud earring in his left ear, a black leather bomber jacket. He cuddled Rhoda into him. 'What am I going to do with you? You know Mum will kill me if she finds out.'

'Better not tell her then,' she said, touching his cheek.

Barney looked at me. 'And I suppose you're the reprobate leading my gran astray,' he said, shaking my hand.

'She doesn't take much leading,' I said.

'You're right there. I'm surprised she's not got a gang of you to escape. Come on, Gran. Let's get you in first.'

Rhoda grabbed his arm, hobbled to the back door of the Range Rover, gave Barney her stick and pulled herself into the back seat.

‘That was easy,’ said Barney. ‘I thought I’d have to lift you in. Looks like I might be going out with Bonnie and Clyde here.’

‘I’m not a crock yet,’ she said. ‘You might need to give Fred a bit of a bum up though. He’s worse on his pins than me.’

He walked back to me. ‘You ready for this,’ he said.

‘I’m ready,’ I said, taking his arm.

We reached the car. I put my foot on the platform, held onto the top of the open door and tried to pull myself in. ‘I think I can do…’

‘None of that,’ said Barney, putting his hands on my backside. ‘Ready. One, two… three.’

He shoved me.

I fell forwards, my head landing in Rhoda’s lap.

‘Oh, my God,’ said Rhoda, throwing her hands in the air. ‘Wait until you’re invited before you start any of that.’

‘Sit up,’ said Barney, grabbing my flailing legs and turning them into the car. ‘There you are. You’re in.’ He slammed the back door shut and got in the driver’s seat. ‘Buckle up back there,’ he said, looking at us in the rear-view mirror. We’ve got a bike to catch.’

I looked behind me as we drove down the hill away from the care home, the stalagmite-shaped glass roof of the communal lounge partially hidden by the Shropshire mist. An architect’s whim to bring in more natural light. I faced Rhoda. ‘You okay?’ I said, squeezing her hand.

‘I’m thinking about Billy,’ she said. ‘He’d have loved this.’

‘He’s still here,’ I said. ‘And he’ll be on the back of that bike with you.’

'Damn right,' said Barney, opening the glove box. He fetched out a silver Buddha-shaped hip flask, reached round and handed it to Rhoda. 'I thought we'd toast Grandad and keep out the cold.'

'You're a soppy old date,' said Rhoda. 'I don't know where you get that from.' She handed me the flask. 'A Christmas present I bought Billy in Cologne,' she said. 'There's an inscription on the back.'

I turned it over. "For my soulmate. Nirvana has its place, but sometimes you need to slug a shot". 'It's lovely,' I said.

'Well, go on then,' said Barney, 'take a drink.'

'Yes,' said Rhoda. 'You go first. Billy would have liked that.'

I unscrewed the top, placed the flask to my lips and drank. Whisky burned the back of my throat. I hated whisky. 'That's hit the spot,' I said, trying not to cough and handing the flask to Rhoda.

She held Buddha in the air. 'Here's to you, Billy,' she said, before taking a long, long slug.

*

Daylight barely lifted as the Range Rover slushed through what seemed like miles and miles of country lanes, the fields whizzing by behind row upon row of hawthorn hedges. Barney chattered away to Rhoda, updating her on family news. 'Mum's got a new bloke,' he said. 'He's alright. We've been out with them a couple of times.'

'Do you see your dad?' said Rhoda.

'Not much. I know Lincoln's not that far away, but it's

not easy to get to. Anyway, I can't talk to that woman he's with now.'

It felt private. I pushed myself away in my head, staring out of the window, concentrating on the hum of the engine.

'Families, eh, Fred,' said Barney. 'I bet your lot are the same.'

'Yes,' I said. 'It's rarely straight forward.'

He smiled at me through the rear-view mirror, encouraging me with his eyes to say more. I couldn't think of anything to say.

'Fred's wife died last year,' said Rhoda. 'His daughter comes to visit him.'

'Yeah,' said Barney. 'We'll have to have a get-together, sort a night out. She married?'

'Yes,' I said. 'She's got two children. Made me a granddad young. They're at university now.'

'Expensive business,' said Barney.

'I've got a son as well,' I said. 'He lives in Spain.'

'I didn't know that,' said Rhoda. 'Billy and I went to Spain a lot. Where does he live?'

'Sitges,' I said. 'He's a lawyer.'

'Sitges,' said Barney. 'That's the gay capital of Europe, isn't it? Don't they have lots of carnivals there?'

'I believe so,' I said. 'I've never been.'

'Sounds wonderful,' said Rhoda. 'A lawyer. That might come in handy. Is he married?'

'No,' I said. 'He lives with someone. They've made a good life out there.' I leaned forward in my seat. 'Is this farm much further?'

'Next turning on the right,' said Barney, looking at me again through the mirror.

*

We turned off the road onto a single-track lane, the branches from the hedges stroking the panels of the Range Rover as we crawled slowly up the hill. Barney turned left at the top and skidded the car to a stop in a clearing. 'There she is,' he said.

I looked out of the window. A man dressed in double denim and sitting on a five-bar fence waved at us. Next to him, propped up on its side stand, stood the most sumptuous looking motorbike I'd ever seen. Barney jumped out the car and hugged the man. They pulled apart and kissed each other on the lips.

'That's Jimmy,' said Rhoda. 'And, yes, they're a couple.'

'I can see that,' I said.

'Does it bother you?'

'Bother me? No. Of course not.'

'It's just, I get the impression your son's gay, and you've never visited.'

'Yes,' I said. 'His mum dealt with all of that.'

'We should go there next. Sitges. You can introduce him to your eccentric girlfriend.'

'You don't believe in beating about the bush, do you? Shall we get this adventure out of the way first?'

'Fair enough. What do you think of the bike?'

'It looks wonderful. Too good to ride.'

'Billy's old bike,' she said. 'A Vincent Black Shadow. It's a collector's item now.'

The back door opened on Rhoda's side. 'Jimmy,' said Barney, 'this is my gran, and that's her sidekick, Fred.'

Jimmy leaned into the car, shook hands with Rhoda

and put his hand up to me. 'You guys must be crazy,' he said.

'And proud of it,' said Rhoda. 'Now, get me out this car. I want to get a closer look at the Shadow.'

'Sure,' said Barney. 'Jimmy, go and get Fred out and we can get started. Careful with him. They've both been at the hip flask.'

Jimmy walked around to my side of the car and opened the door. He held out his hand. I handed him my stick, turned my legs out and crunched my boots into the frozen grass. 'If you can just hold my left arm,' I said, 'I can support my other side with my stick.'

'No problem,' he said. 'You take your time. There's no rush.'

By the time Jimmy had me on my feet, I could see Rhoda standing by the bike. 'You've kept it lovely, Barney,' she said. 'Your granddad would be chuffed to bits.' She reached up and hugged him.

I felt Jimmy's hand on my arm.

'You okay?' he said.

I nodded and we walked over to them, my stick prodding the ground at each step, anchoring my balance.

Rhoda turned to me. 'Isn't it gorgeous?' she said.

I looked at the bike. Highly polished chrome mudguards and exhaust, single football-size globe headlight, a buffed black treacle steel body, accentuated by the white frost background of the landscape. I needed sunglasses to protect me from the glare. 'I have never seen a bike like that,' I said.

'Wait until you see it moving,' said Barney. 'What do you think of the track? Jimmy's had the tractor going round it for two days.'

Rhoda and I looked into the field. Circling the frozen grass was a ploughed-out racing furrow. 'Is it safe?' I said.

'Probably not,' said Barney. 'Jimmy, show them how the bike can handle it.'

Jimmy grinned, jumped on the bike, heeled the side stand clear of the ground, stood up in the saddle and kicked the starting lever, once, nothing, up again, out of the seat, twice, nothing... he shook his head, reached down and fiddled with one of the levers at the side.

'It's cold,' said Barney. 'Just needs a touch more petrol.'

Up went Jimmy again, another kick, nothing, back in the seat, up, another, the bike fired into life, black smoke bellowing out of its exhaust. 'There she blows,' shouted Jimmy, twisting the throttle and scooting the bike into the field. 'Ready,' he said, leaning forwards over the stumpy handlebars, looking at us, twisting the revs up notch after notch.

'Get on with it, Barry Sheen,' said Barney. 'Stop showboating.'

The bike shot forwards.

Rhoda gasped and put her hands to her mouth.

The Shadow streaked around the dirt track as though it had been fired from a cannon, the engine roaring through the gears, Jimmy crouching low, racing style, easing into the circuit, his long blond hair flying in the wind. He screamed as he raced past us. Barney shouted at him to stop, but the exhaust noise from the bike smothered his voice.

Tears rolled down Rhoda's cheeks.

'Are you okay?' I said.

'It's Billy,' she said. 'He looks just like my Billy.'

Jimmy came round again. This time we heard the bike easing down. It stopped in front of us. 'Who's first?' said Jimmy, revving the throttle.

Barney walked over and handed Rhoda the hip flask. 'Drop of Dutch courage,' he said.

'Dutch courage,' said Rhoda, slapping his arm. 'Cheeky young sod. I rode that bike when your mother wasn't even a glint in your granddad's eye.'

'Calm down, Gran,' said Barney. 'I was only—'

'Well don't,' said Rhoda. 'Just get me on the back of the bike. That's if Fred's okay with me going first.'

They all looked at me.

'Yes,' I said. 'Of course.'

Rhoda took Buddha off Barney, took a drink and then handed it to me. 'You can see how safe it is,' she said. 'And have a nip of that. It'll keep your bones warm.'

*

Rhoda had stood her stick against a tree, perched her pom-pom hat and wig on top of a fence post, her strands of grey hair now free to kite-fly from the back of her head as the Shadow raced round the circuit, after circuit, after circuit. Barney and I heard her shouting, 'Again,' each time they came past us, and then, 'Again,' and then, 'Again,' her legs splayed out in front of her, the wind billowing up her dress, her arms gripped in a death vice around Jimmy's body.

Ten minutes later, she climbed off the bike, Barney rushing over to grab her as her feet landed on the grass. 'Gran,' he said. 'Are you okay?'

She bent over, gasping for breath.

'Is she okay?' I shouted. 'That looked bloody terrifying.'

Rhoda stood up straight. 'I'm fucking marvellous,' she screamed to the sky.

Jimmy and Barney laughed.

I hobbled over to her.

'What are you waiting for?' she said. 'Get on the bike.'

'I'm not sure,' I said. 'I don't think I–'

'Barney,' said Rhoda. 'Put him on the bike.'

'Gran, I can't–'

'Put him on the bike,' she said, facing me. 'This is it, Fred. Your chance. It won't come again. Now take a good slug from the flask, get on the bike and hold on for dear life.'

I looked at her. Her eyes pierced into mine.

'Better do as she says, buddy,' said Barney, putting his hand on my arm. 'I'd rather die on the bike than upset her.'

'Do it, Fred,' said Rhoda, grabbing my hand. 'Do it for yourself.'

I unscrewed the top of the hip flask, threw my leg over the Black Shadow and gulped a slug of whisky.

Bug Club

I'm ten when Emma appears in my classroom and changes my life.

She sits at the desk behind me and my best friend, Dee. 'I'm Emma,' she says, clutching my hand and shaking it. 'My dad got a new job. I live here now.'

'What, here?' says Dee. 'At school?'

Emma glares at her. 'I wasn't talking to you,' she says.

The next day, Emma grabs Dee's hair in the dinner queue, pushes her to the floor, kneels down and spits in her face. 'She's mine now,' she says, standing up and putting her arm around me.

Bugs gel us together.

Butterflies, slugs and grasshoppers stick inside jam jars; beetles and spiders scurry through straw. Emma dissects, removes a limb or a wing. 'Oh, my God, that worm's still alive and I've chopped him into three pieces.'

Everywhere I go, she holds my hand, gets in people's faces.

I'm her bug club captain.

She's my protective shadow.

'We don't take any crap,' she says.

My life is better.

Until it isn't.

*

Mum makes me take up Dad's breakfast tray.

His morning fry-up and a bottle of real ale.

I drag my body up the stairs, smelling the filth from his bedroom as I reach the top of the landing. His room is in darkness, the curtains permanently closed with a safety pin. Mum used to come in here once a year to give him sex on his birthday. Sometimes she'd be back in the kitchen before her coffee had gone cold, still wearing her housework apron.

She doesn't do that anymore.

'Pop it down there, sweetheart,' he says, as I reach the bedroom door. He nods towards the bedside table.

'I need to go to school, Dad. I'll miss the bus.'

'I know, but you can stay for a couple of minutes.'

I put the tray down.

'Shut the door,' he says.

Run, run, run. I freeze. Perhaps this is how it has to be, how dads are. Mum knows best. If it's wrong, Mum would stop it. 'You're a big girl now. Daddy's big girl.'

I hear him pat the bed. 'Come and lie with your old dad for a bit.'

Afterwards, all I see in my head are his bear-like hands, hard skin, farm grimy, dirt under his fingernails. The after-smell of his stale sweat roots in my nostrils. I brush my teeth, go back downstairs, pick up my Scooby-Doo lunchbox, throw my school satchel over my shoulder and walk towards the back door, conscious that the bus is due any minute.

'Have a nice day at school,' says Mum, her back to me, standing at the Belfast sink, looking out into the garden, two boiled eggs bubbling on the stove next to her.

I glare at her and open the back door.

*

Cockroaches.

Emma's obsession at thirteen.

Scuttling, slimy, hard-cased leather shells, long, threadlike antennae probing out a survival route. The damp farmhouse kitchen floor evolves a tide, a black carpet mass of undulating bodies, like a Vincent Price tea party. And then, when you switch on the light, they swarm for the covers, disappear under the washing machine, cooker, drier and skirting boards.

We watch as the roaches weave through the straw-filled olive jars we keep in my dad's barn. Emma lets three of them scuttle over her hands, drops them on the floor and stamps on them. Crunch. Crunch. Crunch. 'Listen to that,' she screams. 'Breaking bones. I love that noise.'

'You know their eggs are stuck to your shoe now,' I say.

'What?'

'It's true. They're survival ninjas. The only insects to have survived the ice-age.'

Emma nods, picks up another, squeezes it between her fingers, close to her face. She's staring straight at its antennae. 'They can survive a week without their head,' she says, mushing the cockroach's head between her fingers and dropping its body to the floor.

I stamp on it. Crunch. 'No need to be cruel,' I say.

'You know you can bring them back to life.'

'What?'

She nods towards the chest freezer. 'I've been experimenting. You can thaw them out and away they scuttle.'

'You worry me.'

'You love it. I'll tell you something else, but it's a bit gory.'

'What's new?' I say.

'Human bodies. You can store them. It's easy. You just need a maggot bath to eat away the flesh and an acid drip to strip the bones. All you're left with is the skeleton. It only takes a couple of months for each one.'

'And then what? Hang them in a cupboard?'

'Well, everyone needs a few skeletons in their cupboard.'

'You are completely bonkers,' I say.

'Loveable with it,' she says, hugging me close.

*

I'm fifteen when cancer takes my revenge on Mum.

I hide her morphine, listen to her screaming from her room at the back of the house. A substitute. That's what she made me. Called me off the bench to do her dirty work. Some nights I sit in her room, watching her in the dark, turning a carving knife over and over in my hands. She keeps her eyes open, waiting for the release, neither of us saying a word. Cancer rips away at her for a year before she dies.

It's not long enough.

I clear the breakfast tray with a single arm sweep, hold the same carving knife to Dad's throat. 'If you touch me again, I'll slit you open.'

He nods. Scared eyes looking down at the blade, tears streaming down his cheeks. 'You're hurting me, sweetheart.'

I look at the knife. Blood trickles towards his grey chest hairs. I want to push. I force myself to pull away.

'You should have gushed him,' says Emma. 'Set him off like a fountain.'

I shake my head. 'He's still my dad.'

The next morning Emma races into the kitchen carrying his favourite axe, the one with an oak handle and a carving of a woodman. I follow her upstairs and watch from the landing as she bursts into Dad's room, raises the axe above her head and crashes it into Dad's face. I walk over to the bed and look at him. His nose is split in two. I wonder if he felt anything. It takes both of us to pull the axe out. We drag him downstairs, letting his head bang on every step, out through the kitchen, across the courtyard and into the barn.

That's when our new collection starts.

*

From the perimeter fence we watch the already crowded fair, the steaming May temperature bringing out the sweat-vested, denim-shorted, buttock-baring locals. 'Jesus,' says Emma, 'there are some sights in there.'

'Yes,' I say, shading my eyes. 'It looks like the hillbillies are in town. Let's go see what we can find.'

We walk across the grass. I feel drops of sweat dripping down my back. I pull my thin cotton, sleeveless dress away from my legs. 'I can't believe this heat.'

Emma grabs my hand and we run into the hub of the fair, the Boomtown Rats, "I Don't Like Mondays" bangs out of the stereo system; the smell of fried onions and doughnuts laces the air. I pull Emma to a standstill. 'Bumper cars or Waltzers?' I say, looking straight into her eyes.

She turns my head towards the Waltzers. A gypsy-hair, blue-eyed cute boy swings off the back of a car and waves at us. I wave back and then squeeze Emma's hand. 'I'm so jealous of your radar,' I say. 'He's perfect.'

We drop into the nearest car. Cute boy jumps on the back and grins. He has a red-faced pirate tattoo on his forearm. 'You two okay?' he says.

'I am now,' I say, looking up at him. 'Are you going to stay there?'

'If you want.'

*

The Waltzer comes to a standstill after five minutes of whirling and screaming. We climb out, fall off the wooden platform and onto the grass. Emma hugs me and strides off towards the ghost train. 'See you later, Captain,' she shouts, putting her hand in the air.

'Captain?' says cute boy, giving me a puzzled look.

'It's a private joke,' I say, pushing my hair off my face. 'Not funny really.'

'I'm Steve,' he says.

'Jo-Jo,' I say.

'So, Jo-Jo, if you can wait ten minutes, I'll show you the fair.'

'Do I get a candyfloss?'

'You can have a bucketload.'

'In that case, I'll wait.'

*

Bang.

I scream and clap. 'Three to go,' I shout.

Steve lifts his head off the rifle butt, looks up at me and winks. 'Don't worry,' he says. 'That bear's as good as yours.'

I stroke the top of his thigh through his Brutus jeans. 'I never doubted it for a second,' I whisper in his ear.

'You have to get all six for the bear,' says the Shoot a Duck man.

'I know, Harry. I've worked here long enough. And I want the big bear, not the puny thing you give to punters.'

'The sign says win a bear,' says Harry. 'It don't specify a size.'

'Yeah,' says Steve, closing his one eye and squeezing the trigger. 'You can explain that to me later if you want.'

*

I cuddle the snow-white bear into my chest as we walk away from the stall. Steve has his hand in the middle of my back. I pray my dress isn't damp from my sweat. 'Didn't you promise me a candyfloss?' I say, turning to face him.

'Are you always so bossy?'

'You'll get used to me.'

'Okay. I'll get you a candyfloss.'

I drop the bear on the grass, put my arms around Steve's neck and pull him towards me. 'Do you want your reward here?' I say.

'My reward?'

'For winning me the bear.'

He blushes and looks around the fairground.

So cute. I nearly changed my mind. 'Or we could go somewhere more private,' I say.

*

I skid my red Ford Capri off the gravel car park.

Steve grips the side of his seat. 'Do you always drive so fast?' he says.

'I thought someone with a pirate tattoo would like adventure.'

He touches his arm and traces his finger around the skull and crossbones. 'Drunken night out. Seemed like a good idea after half a bottle of Southern Comfort.'

'How long have you worked at the fair?'

'Just this summer.'

'It must be exciting, meeting different people every night.'

'Yeah. A new town every couple of weeks. It suits me.'

'And a new girl?'

'Not really.'

'Sure. I believe you.'

'What about you?'

'Oh, boring, boring. Shop assistant, live alone.'

'Your mate seems like fun.'

'Emma. We've been best friends since junior school.'

'What's the captain thing about?'

'It's silly. When we were kids we belonged to a bug club, collecting insects in jars. I was the captain. It sort of stuck.'

'Didn't the bugs just die?'

'Not straight away. We put air holes in the lids.'

*

We drive through country lanes for about twenty minutes, neither of us saying a word for the last five. I think about Emma, about the farm, the collection. Emma says we need to move on, find a bigger place. She's keen to expand.

'Where are we going?' says Steve.

'I wondered when you were going to ask.'

'You seem trustworthy,' he says, putting his hand on my leg.

I look down at his hand, which is half on my dress and half on my bare thigh. He catches me looking, blushes again and puts his hand back on his leg. 'That's your dick talking?' I say. 'You've only just met me.'

'No. I'm a good judge of character. I have a knack for it.'

'Yeah. Tell me what you think you know.'

'About what?'

'About me. If you're that good, it should be easy.'

'Well, you've got kind eyes–'

'–everyone says that. When you ask them what they think of you, they always say something nice about your eyes. It doesn't mean anything.'

'Okay. You like candyfloss and big cuddly bears. How can that be wrong?'

'So, even Hitler liked watercolours.'

'You still haven't said where we're going.'

'My place.'

'You must live in the sticks?'

'My dad was a farmer.'

'Was?'

'He's dead.'

'I'm sorry.'

'It's okay. Mum's dead as well. Like I said, I live on my own.'

*

I turn right off the main road, drive down a conifer-hedged country lane and into a driveway sweep in front of a four-bedroomed detached house. I pull hard on the handbrake and switch off the engine. 'Here we are,' I say. 'Back at the ranch.'

'Wow,' says Steve. 'It's huge. Is it all yours?'

'Yeah. Every single tin-roofed outbuilding. Dad was very generous.'

'It must be worth a fortune.'

'I've not thought about it.'

He leans across and kisses me. 'Are you sure about this, Jo-Jo? We've only just met. I don't want to rush you.'

'I'm sure. Are you?'

'Yeah,' he says, kissing me again. 'I've got a good feeling about us.'

I pat his thigh. 'That's good. Me too. Let's get inside.'

*

We walk hand in hand towards the front door, leaving the bear on the back seat.

I put my key in the lock and face him. 'Close your eyes,' I say.

'What?'

'Close your eyes. I want to guide you in.'

'You're kidding.'

'It'll be fun. I thought you trusted me.'

'I do, but… oh, okay.'

I push the door open and lead him into the house. 'No peeking,' I say.

'I feel ridiculous,' he says.

I kiss him lightly on the lips. 'Nearly there. Only two more steps. One, two.' I let go of his hands and step back. 'Open your eyes,' I shout.

'What the…'

Emma fires a bullet into his head.

*

We stand side by side in the barn, sipping our coffee.

I hear the rain bouncing off the barn roof. There's a lingering smell of cow shit and rotting flesh. Olive jars and fish tanks are piled high next to bales of straw against the wooden wall. 'Are you okay?' says Emma, putting her arm around me.

'I was thinking about Mum,' I say.

'Her. Good riddance.'

'I know, but—'

'But nothing. She was garbage. You've got me now. At least she got a proper burial.'

I look down at the horse trough. Some of the maggots have wriggled over the edge and are escaping across the floor. Steve's body is smothered. Emma walks over to a metal cupboard and opens the doors; four skeletons draped over wooden coat hangers swing out at her. 'Be good to get some more company for these,' she says.

I walk over, reach out and touch Dad's skull.

'Dirty old bastard,' says Emma.

'Yeah,' I say, taking a sip of my coffee. I look back at the horse trough. 'That one was cute.'

'Still a man,' says Emma.

'We've come a long way since bug club,' I say. 'How many do you think it'll take?'

She shrugs. 'Until it stops being fun, I guess. And then we'll find something else.'

I throw the dregs of my coffee onto the barn floor. 'Let's go and get something to eat.'

'Aye, aye, Captain,' she says.

'Do you mean that?' I say.

'Of course I do,' she says, reaching up and touching my cheek. 'I'm nothing without you.'

We walk out of the barn arm in arm.

Miss Denny's Captain

May 1848.

Upstairs, next to the loom, in her Barnham Broom cottage, Mum lay on a stump bedstead, a few stretched cords and a coarse sack filled with straw supporting her ravaged body. A single woollen blanket covered her, which she said made her itch.

'I don't know what to do, Mum,' I said.

She grabbed my hand, tried to say something, but the consumption squeezed her lungs and stole her breath.

Her skin felt hot and clammy.

I leaned forward.

'Take these,' she whispered, sliding a pocket-size hessian bag from under the blanket.

She coughed again and gulped in mouthfuls of air.

'Mum,' I said.

She tried to smile. Her eyes watered. 'Go and find yourself a new life,' she said.

*

I watched as the wharfinger counted out my six shillings and sixpence fare. 'All there,' he said, placing the money in a brass tin and locking it away in his desk drawer. He nodded at my mum's carpet bag. 'Is that all you're taking?'

'Yes,' I said, looking over at the blond-haired clerk who was sitting at a desk in a corner of the cabin.

The clerk blushed when I met his eyes.

I turned back to the wharfinger. 'This boat you're putting me on, they're respectable people?'

'They're churchgoers, Miss Denny, when they get the chance.'

'Good. My mum wouldn't want me getting on a boat with drunks.'

We strode along the boardwalk, the wharfinger leading the way. I trod carefully, conscious of the loose stitches holding together my handmade boots.

The wharf bustled with narrowboats, all with garishly painted rudders and tillers, some with fancy white ropework bedecking their hulls. Boatmen wearing thick leather belts and sleeved waistcoats hauled hessian sacks off the dock and onto the decks. They stopped for a moment to nudge each other as I walked by.

I pulled my carpet bag closer to me and kept my gaze fixed on the wharfinger's back as he strode out our route. 'Here she is,' he said, stopping in front of a boat painted with images of yellow, blue and red shooting stars, its name on its side in duck-egg blue letters – Poseidon's Quest.

'Captain John,' shouted the wharfinger.

*

Three days into the journey, I sat on the deck, my legs dangling towards the canal, Captain John at the tiller, smoking his clay pipe and steering our twisting path along the cut.

His nephew, Thomas, walked along the towpath behind two donkeys, Martha and Gert. Martha hee-hawed her disapproval when Thomas patted her backside. 'She's not happy with you,' shouted John.

Thomas turned his head towards the boat. 'She wants her feed, Uncle. So do I.'

'Only a couple more miles to our stop,' said John, tapping his pipe on the cabin roof to liven up the tobacco. 'You okay up there, Phil? Don't you go falling in.'

I smiled at him, and he winked.

I looked down at the still water. Mum's owl eyes bounced back.

She'd left me thirty shillings and a letter from her brother, Arthur, a master tailor in Whitham, containing his offer to take me on as an apprentice. She'd also left me her clothes. Two high-necked, round-collar blouses, long sleeves ballooning out at the forearm, coming to a tight cuff at the wrist, and two bell-shaped skirts, which skimmed the floor when I walked, picking up the dust, mud or whatever else I dragged across on my travels. All were ink-blue and made out of thick cotton, which anchored me down in the wet and sweated me up like a carthorse in the heat. They hadn't needed much alteration, but I now spent my life sewing and repairing, making sure they made it through another day.

I thought about Hettie, my little sister, four years old, clutching her grubby rag doll, both her parents dead. I hoped she'd be okay with Auntie Lil.

'Do you want to steer for a bit?' shouted John.

I nodded, stood up, walked across the deck and dropped down beside him. He touched my face. I could smell the tangy pungency of his fresh working-day sweat. 'You look gorgeous,' he said. 'The sun's brought all your freckles out.'

I glanced at the bank.

Thomas had his back to us, still moaning at Martha.

I pulled John's head down and kissed him on the lips. He put my hand on the tiller. 'None of that,' he said. 'You've got to keep this boat in deep water.'

An hour later, we moored up. Thomas unclipped Martha and Gert's harnesses and dragged them off towards the stable on the far side of the wharf. 'Make sure he gives them decent oats this time,' shouted John. 'He's a tight git that ostler, and they need their strength.'

'Do you want me to get them shoed?' said Thomas.

'That'll wait,' said John. 'We'll do it tomorrow.'

He turned to me as Thomas disappeared over the bank. 'Now,' he said, 'I think you owe me a cuddle.'

'Oh, do I?' I said. 'Well maybe cuddling time has passed you by.'

He scooped me up in his arms and carried me into his cabin at the stern of the boat. The master's suite he called it. We lay down on the single wooden bed, me with my head on his chest, looking up at him. He had cobalt-blue eyes and a tightly cropped black beard. I snuggled into him. He made me feel like I was with a high-seas adventurer who would swim across oceans to bring me home. He lifted my head and kissed me.

'You taste of salt and tobacco,' I said.

He laughed. 'It must be the old sea dog coming out in me.'

I reached down and unfastened his thick leather belt. 'Yes,' I said. 'It must.'

*

I'd been lying on the deck for an hour, my blouse stuck to my body. I'd removed the detachable sleeves, giving my naked arms access to the light breath of a cool breeze coming off the water.

I stared up at the cloudless sky, trying to count the stars, listening to the narrowboat straining on its mooring, its timbers creaking underneath me, the hull complaining about being tied up, wanting to get going again, get on with the job of traversing the seemingly endless path through the winding route of the canal.

It had been four days since I met my captain, hours spent watching him at the tiller, his sleeves rolled up, his muscular arms steering the narrowboat through the murky water of the cut, him barking out instructions to Thomas who kept his eyes fixed on the backsides of Martha and Gert as they grudgingly plodded out their long days of tedious drudgery along the towpath.

There were moments of difference.

The time when a barge came from the opposite direction, its lumbering grey shire horse nudging our donkeys to the bank side of the towpath, John slowing the boat in response to the warning sound of the oncoming captain's smacking whip – short handles, a thin-plaited cotton lash, a silk thrum on the end to make the thunder crack echo.

Thomas halted the donkeys at the sound of the lash, and John wrapped the towline two or three times around a wooden strapping post set firmly in the canal side of the bank, slowing the momentum of Poseidon's Quest. The two captains nodded at each other as the shire horse dragged the Aphrodite's Sceptre past our shooting-stars-emblazoned hull, Thomas left to persuade Martha and Gert to lean into their holsters and stretch the cotton strap taut. The donkeys' continuous tug, tug, tugging eventually overcame the inertia of thirty tonnes and, with more smacking and shouting from Thomas, and lots of hee-hawing from Martha, the boat's pace ratcheted up until we reached full speed.

And then there were the bridges, low and numerous, no towpath underneath, the traverse through negotiated by John and Thomas lying on a plank across the bow of the boat, legging the momentum by pushing with their feet against the tunnel walls.

These distractions passed the daylight hours, but I lived for my night-time satisfaction, snuggled up in John's arms, my head on his chest, him stroking my hair, telling me it was all going to be okay.

'Hello, miss.'

'Thomas,' I said, sitting up and straightening my dress. 'I didn't hear you.'

'I needed to get out of that cabin,' he said, nodding towards the bow of the boat. 'I'm boiling in there. It's like hell itself.'

He sat down next to me, and we stared in silence at the water.

'It's a lovely night,' I said, suddenly realising I'd left my boots off and my bare feet were poking out from under my skirt. I tried to curl them out of sight.

'It's going to be hot tomorrow,' he said. 'That'll not please the donkeys.'

'They do give you some grief. Do you hate them?'

'Not really. Don't reckon I'd be too happy if I had to tug this thing about.'

'No,' I said. 'I don't think I would either.'

He reached into his pocket, pulled out a bracelet of brown beads and turned them over in his hand. He must have felt me watching. 'My dad's worry beads,' he said. 'They help me relax.'

'I've got a lace handkerchief of my mum's,' I said. 'It still smells of her lavender perfume, helps bring her back.'

'John's been good to me,' he said, passing the beads through his fingers. 'Took me in when Mum and Dad passed on. I'd have been in the workhouse if it weren't for him.'

'He's a good man,' I said.

'Yeah, him and Auntie Barbara have seen me right. I'd hate to see anything come between them.'

He pushed the worry beads back into his trouser pocket and stood up. 'It'll be morning soon. I'd better head off to the stables and wake Martha and Gert.'

*

Darkness lifted; a light mist hovered over the surface of the cut.

I stood up, jumped off the boat, padded along the bank to the long grass at the side of the lock, pulled up my skirt, crouched down and relieved myself. I straightened my clothes and walked back along the towpath.

John waved at me from the deck of Poseidon's Quest. 'Where've you been?' he shouted. 'I woke up and the boat was deserted. I thought there'd been a mutiny.'

I grabbed his hand and jumped back on board.

'Where are your shoes?' he said.

'Tell me about Barbara,' I said.

He turned away, picked up one of the donkey's harnesses off the cabin roof and unfastened the buckle holding together the leather straps.

'Is she your wife?' I said.

He put the harness on the deck and stared at the water. 'Yes,' he said.

'And when were you going to tell me?'

'I've tried, but I didn't know how to start. It doesn't have to change anything.'

'It changes everything, John.'

He grabbed my arm. 'She doesn't want me. I don't want her.'

'Till death you do part,' I said. 'Or have you forgotten that bit?'

'She won't care as long as I look after her and the kids.'

'You've got children?'

He looked at the water again. 'Two boys,' he said.

I pulled away from him, walked into the cabin, sat on the bed and stared through the open door. I could hear birdsong. My mind felt numb. A wife. Children. He had a life.

I heard John's voice. 'What have you been telling her?'

'Nothing you shouldn't have told her already.'

I jumped off the bed and went back on deck.

Thomas stood on the towpath, Martha and Gert hee-hawing at his side.

John went to step off the boat and onto the bank. His face was florid.

'John,' I shouted.

'I'm sorry,' he said, turning and looking at me.

'He should've told you,' said Thomas, tears streaming down his cheeks.

John ran over to me and pulled me into his chest. I could hear his heart racing. 'Please can we try and make this work,' he said.

*

The narrowboat's early morning shadow loomed across the water, almost touching the opposite bank. Thomas had tied Martha and Gert to a strapping post before he'd walked away up the hill. Martha nibbled Gert's back. Gert had her head down, munching at a stray clump of grass.

John and I sat side by side on deck. 'Do you need to go after him?' I said.

'He's angry,' said John. 'So am I. We need to calm down.'

'He's right though. You should have told me.'

'I wanted to, but it all happened so quickly. One minute you were throwing your bag onboard and the next we were in bed.'

'But afterwards, you should have told me then.'

'I didn't want to lose you,' he said, wiping the tears off his face. 'I still don't.'

'You're married.'

'Does that mean I can't be happy?'

'It means you've made vows. Solemn vows.'

'You don't want me.'

'I can't have you, John. You belong to someone else.'

I stood up, walked up the deck a few paces and then turned back towards him. 'We made a mistake,' I said. 'I'm leaving. I'll find another boat.'

'No,' he said, jumping to his feet. 'I want to marry you. I want us to be together, to have a family.'

'You're already married. You already have a family.'

He grabbed my arms. 'What does that matter?'

'You can't divorce her. You'll never get a divorce.'

'We'll get married somewhere else. No one will know. I'll see them right. You could come and live with us, come away with me on boat trips. We'd have a good life.'

'That's not the life I want. How can you even suggest that?'

'We can make it work.'

'It's over, John. You need to go back to your family.'

'Please,' he said. 'Don't leave me.'

I walked into the cabin, closed the door, pulled my carpet bag from under the single bed and threw in my clothes. I wanted to punch the wall. Marriage. I had this vision of me and her sat opposite each other in some dank kitchen, rocking away the time in our chairs, probably crocheting.

I blew my nose on Mum's lace handkerchief, lay down on the bed and closed my eyes.

*

I sat on the bank, in-between my captain's legs, my feet dangling in the water.

'Shall we go in,' he whispered, nuzzling the back of my neck.

I turned my head and kissed him.

'I love you,' he said.

We dropped off the side, his arms wrapping me tight as the water surged up my naked body. I reached behind me and grabbed the back of his bare thighs. He placed his hands on my hips and turned me towards him. We faced each other, rising through the water, the sunlight on the surface coming closer and closer. We broke through into the open air. I gasped. He gasped. 'That was great,' he said. 'Shall we do it again.'

'Promise me you'll never leave me,' I said.

'I promise' he said.

We scrambled back up the bank, faced the canal and held hands.

'One, two, three,' he shouted.

We jumped.

I woke up.

The boat was moving.

I turned off the bed, opened the door and walked onto the deck.

John stood at the tiller.

'What are you doing?' I said.

'We'll be in Whitham by nightfall,' he said. 'There's no sense in you paying out for another boat.'

I looked at the bank. Martha and Gert were back in their harnesses, plodding out our route, Thomas behind them, his head bowed.

John picked up his pipe from the cabin roof and turned it over in his hand. 'We've not been intimate for years,' he said. 'Me and the wife. I want you to know that.'

I heard a screech from the cut. A gaggle of swans swam in front of us, a cob, a pen, six cygnets, a perfect line, adults front and back, babies in the middle, the convoy pushing through the water and down the side of the boat.

Mum's words dropped into my head. 'Go and find yourself a new life.'

I held my stomach.

'I would look after you,' said John.

I stood by his side at the tiller and touched his face. 'I know you will,' I said.

Finding Tommy and Archie

Tommy watched the luminous red digits on the alarm clock drop down the minutes until they landed on midnight. He lay on his back, pulled the green woollen blanket up under his chin and stared at the ceiling. 'Happy birthday, Archie,' he said, rubbing his eyes and reaching over to switch on the tiffany shade lamp at the side of his bed.

He picked up the birthday card from the bedside cabinet, rested his back against the headboard and read the message out loud, "Happy Birthday, Tommy. All my love, Mum".

Two brothers, the same birthday, ten years between them.

Tommy threw the card to the floor.

Dad. 26 April 1970. Dead at forty-five. Archie. 5 May 1970. Dead at seventeen.

Ten years ago, but it still felt like a free fall into a black hole.

'Jesus, Archie. Why? Just tell me why.'

He heard the bedroom chair scrape on the floorboards.

A woman stood by the door.

She wore a navy-blue trouser suit and red pixie boots.

Tommy tried to turn out of bed, but he couldn't move – his legs felt like they'd been superglued to the mattress. 'Who are you?' he said. 'What are you doing in my house?'

'I'm not going to hurt you, Tommy,' she said before turning and pressing her lips against the wall at the foot of his bed. 'We're ready to begin,' she whispered.

Bang!

A chasm opened up in the plaster, yawning its way to the skirting boards, the door frame and the edge of the ceiling. 'What the hell is that?' said Tommy, trying in vain to peel his body off the mattress.

The woman floated over to him and massaged his right temple, her chocolate-brown irises acting as a magnet and drawing his attention. 'I've been watching over you for a long time, Tommy. I'm going to help you understand.'

She clicked her fingers. A mercury-coloured liquid, sparking with electric charge, bubbled to the surface of the chasm, flowed over the ragged edges and covered the full length of his bedroom wall. 'You can get up now,' she said.

He tried to move his legs again. This time they came free. He rolled to a sitting position and stood up. The room rocked from side to side. 'Get your balance,' she said, putting her hand on his arm, the giddiness washing away as soon as she touched him.

Tommy looked again at the wall. Ripples of mercury tapped against each other, sending sparks of blue electric charge pinging from its surface. He walked over to the torn plaster. 'Touch it,' she said. He dipped his right hand in the liquid. It felt like hot sand. He pulled his hand out. Bone dry. 'I've never seen anything like it,' he said.

The woman guided him back to the bed. 'Sit down,' she said.

Tommy dropped onto the mattress, and she knelt in front of him.

'I'm here to answer your questions about Archie,' she said.

He looked around the room, half expecting to see his big brother grinning at him from the shadows. 'You've spoken to him?' he said.

She nodded.

'That's impossible. This is a sick joke.'

He tried to stand, but his bare feet slipped on the nylon carpet, and he fell back on the bed.

The woman leaned forward. 'Trust me,' she whispered in his right ear. 'Trust me.'

*

Wake up, Tommy. Wake up.

Tommy stood at the side of the pine dining table in the kitchen of their council house in Severn Road and watched as Archie dipped the rubber inner tube of a bicycle tyre in a washing up bowl full of water, moving it around underneath the surface, carefully examining each section. Tommy looked up at him. 'It's there,' said Archie, showing him a split in the rubber. 'You see the air bubbles? We just need to pop on a patch, and it'll be as good as new.' Archie dried the inner tube on one of their mum's tea towels, opened up a red oblong tin and fetched out a tube of glue. 'Won't be long now,' he said. 'We'll soon have you back on the road.'

Wake up, Tommy. Wake up.

Tommy sat on the side of the pool at the Gala Swimming Baths in Walsall, his feet in the water. He held his arms out in front of him. Archie floated out a few feet, the water up to his chest. 'Go on,' said Archie. 'Just fall in. And remember to hold your breath.' Tommy hesitated, dropped off the side and hit the water with a scream. Archie's arms wrapped around him and guided him to the surface. 'That was great,' Tommy spluttered. 'Can I do it again?'

'Yeah,' said Archie, grinning at him.

Wake up, Tommy. Wake up.

Tommy opened his eyes.

The woman had propped him up in bed, his head resting on three duck-feather pillows. 'It's okay,' she said, wiping his forehead with a white cotton handkerchief. 'It'll get better the longer I spend with you.'

He looked at the wall. The ripples of plasma were still knocking against each other. He squeezed the woman's hand. 'This must be a dream,' he said.

'It's no dream, Tommy. I'm here to help you understand.'

'You said you'd spoken to Archie.'

She clicked her fingers again.

The mercury swirled in concentric circles, clearing with each revolution, sucking itself to the edges of the wall, leaving behind a new image, a beach, an azure sea, a boat chugging along the horizon, and a man with his back to the bedroom, sitting on the sand, staring out at the falling sun as it melted into the ocean. 'Look closely,' said the woman.

The wall zoomed in on the man.

He wore a red check lumberjack shirt.

*

Archie sat on a cast-iron park bench next to a wood of eucalyptus trees, behind him a meadow of purple and white rhododendron bushes. The sweet scent of their blossoms filled his nostrils, making him feel slightly nauseous. In front of him was a millpond, in its centre two naked nymph statues, a boy and a girl, holding hands, a fountain of water gushing from each of their mouths.

The only sound he could hear was the splash and plop of the fountains.

'Hello, Archie.'

A woman's voice.

He couldn't see anyone, but he felt a hand squeeze his right hand.

Archie stood up, allowing himself to be led away along the bank of the pond and up a dirt track. At the summit of a hill, he reached a second cast-iron bench overlooking the water. 'You need to wait here,' said the voice.

'When will you be back?'

'When you're ready.'

He sat down and stared at the view. The moribund millpond, sunrise, sunset, the night after night return of a circle of fruit bats seeking out a sleeping refuge, the evergreen rhododendron bushes, the spurting nymphs, twisting banners of ghost dancing mist, moonbeams clasping the water, the wood of eucalyptus trees stretching itself higher and higher towards the heavens.

On and on time went.

He never shifted his position, his eyes focused, his mind trying to remember, trying to work it out. And slowly, very slowly, it came back… who he was, how he'd come to be here. 'Oh my God,' he screamed.

'Hello,' said the voice.

*

Archie saw a woman standing on the opposite side of the hill's summit. She faced him, her hands on her hips. He struggled to hold her in focus. He squinted, but it made things worse. One moment she was there, and he could see her blue trouser suit and red pixie boots, the next she was fudged, or bits of her, a leg, an arm, were missing.

And then she was at his side, her hand on his shoulder. 'It'll take a few moments to adjust,' she said.

He put his hands over his eyes and cried. She put her arm around him and rubbed the top of his back. He eased away from her, reached into his pocket, pulled out a paper tissue and blew his nose. 'Am I dead?' he said.

'Come with me,' she said, holding out her hand.

She pulled him away from the bench.

Archie walked through a new avenue, this time made up of coconut palms and mango trees, his bare feet dusted with each step by talcum powder sand. At the end of the avenue, the trunks of two trees grew into each other, forming a natural archway and a frame for the vista of an ocean. He walked closer and closer to the sea, mesmerised by the sunlight sparkling off the water, tasting the salty air, smelling the heady citrus aroma of the plants.

He stepped through the archway and, for a moment, he stopped breathing.

The woman let go of his hand and he stood perfectly

still, the infinity view of azure sea emptying his thoughts and shutting his mind into silence. He could hear the lap of the waves as they kissed the white sand shore, softly caressing, rolling backwards, forwards, backwards, forwards. He looked at the ocean, a small boat chugging along the horizon his only point of reference. The boat reached the periphery of his view, looked like it was in danger of falling off the edge of the world, and then turned around, crawling back on itself again and again, marking time, ticking away the revolutions.

Archie looked back towards the path. Crab tracks covered the beach and, next to his, a set of human footprints leading up and away from the archway.

The woman had disappeared.

He sat down on the sand and waited.

*

He'd lost track of the number of sunrises and sunsets he'd lived through since the woman had left him with nothing but the lapping tranquillity of the ocean's waves. *Lived through.* He let the words tumble across his mind. 'You're dead,' he told himself.

He focused again on the horizon.

The boat had disappeared.

'Hello,' said the woman.

She sat down next to him, picked up a small piece of sun-bleached coral and turned it over in her left hand. He looked at the light cyan blue of the lagoon and followed its trail beyond the reef to the inky dark of the deep. 'What is this place?' he said.

'Limbo,' she said. 'It's a sort of waiting room. The way you came here wasn't right, Archie. You've left a lot of people wanting to know why.'

He grabbed a handful of sand and let it slide through his fingers. 'You mean my family.'

'I mean your brother.'

'Tommy. He's just a kid.'

She threw the coral into the ocean, rubbed her hands together to brush off the sand and stood up. 'He's looking for answers. Answers only you can give him.'

Archie felt the tears tracking down his cheeks. She knelt down and hugged him.

She smelt of pine needles.

*

Archie and the woman walked in silence off the beach, through the archway, back along the avenue of coconut palms and mango trees, up the dirt track and down the hill. They reached the first cast-iron bench and sat down. The millpond, the rhododendron bushes, the gushing nymph statues, the eucalyptus trees – they were all exactly as he'd left them.

The woman squeezed his hand.

'I need to talk to him,' he said. 'To explain what happened.'

'You can't go back,' she said.

'Then how can I answer his questions?'

'You can let him watch what you know, what you remember.'

'I don't understand,' he said.

She pointed at the millpond. 'He's watching us now,' she said.

*

Tommy sat propped up in bed, his head resting against the headboard.

The mercury screen juddered into a still frame, leaving Archie and the woman sitting on a cast-iron bench, looking at a millpond, frozen in time. 'But that's you,' he said. 'How can you be in two places at once?'

'I'm not really in either place, Tommy.'

He touched her arm. 'You're here. I can feel you.'

'I'm also with Archie.'

He looked again at the screen. A fop of jet-black hair, a lopsided grin, acne scars on his cheeks. 'I can't believe I'm looking at him. I've missed him so much. Can I talk to him?'

The woman put her hand on Tommy's shoulder, sending a tingle of warmth through his body. 'He's dead,' she said. 'But he wants to explain.'

'How can he do that if I can't talk to him?'

'He can show you his memory of the day he died.'

Tommy felt a knot tighten in his stomach. 'I'm not sure I can cope with that,' he said.

The woman pointed at the screen.

*

'You look after your mother, laddie. You're the man of the house now.'

Dr Dwyer, grey worsted suit, trilby hat, omnipresent stethoscope around his neck. Archie's family doctor, known for his quick temper and making you feel guilty for daring to mention your ailments. For the last year, he'd drunk their teapot dry – three sugars and a spot of milk – eaten their mum's nutmeg-covered egg custards, munched his way through their biscuit barrel – especially the ginger nuts – and battled the dare-not-speak-its-name Big C being chased by the surgeons around their dad's battered body.

'He will, Doctor,' said their mum, wiping her eyes with a scrunched-up white lace handkerchief she'd had balled in her fist for most of the morning. 'He's a good boy.'

'And that little brother of yours. What have you done with him today?'

'He's with Miss Reece,' said their mum.

'Aye,' he said. 'This is no place for kiddies. Miss Reece will see him right. I'll pop and see you tomorrow, and don't forget what I've told you about those tablets, missus.'

He opened the front door and stepped out into the street.

'Thank you for coming,' said their mum. 'It's very good of you.'

He threw a hand in the air and walked off down the drive.

Their mum gave one final wave, closed the front door and burst into tears.

Archie hugged her, desperately searching the fog inside his brain for something to say. He needed his dad to ruffle his hair and sort it all out. He put his head on his mum's shoulder and cried. She patted his back. 'It'll be okay, Archie,' she said. 'It'll be okay.'

Archie eased away from her. 'It's never going to be okay,' he said.

'No,' she said, touching his face.

His mum wiped her eyes and looked up at their dad's faded black-and-white photo, hanging on the hallway wall. Their dad at seventeen, before his navy adventures around the globe, his wild, sandy hair sticking out in all directions, the wide collar of his rain mac pulled up, a wool scarf wrapped tightly around his neck. It looked like he'd gone into the photobooth to shelter from the wind. 'I need to talk to you, Archie,' his mum said. 'And I need you to be strong.'

*

Archie drove down Berwick Road, the conversation with his mum looping inside his head.

She came to see you a couple of times, but you were a baby, and she had all those kiddies of his... you were only one. She couldn't have kept you.

He dropped the Ford Anglia into second gear and counted down the numbers. Twenty-eight, twenty-six, twenty-four... twenty-two. He pulled on the handbrake and turned off the engine.

I can't believe you never told me, Mum.

It doesn't make a difference. You're still my son.

Archie crunched up the gravel path, stood on the step and went to press the doorbell, but someone knocked on the bay window.

A florid-cheeked man stared out at him, dressed in a collarless white shirt and pinstripe trousers held up by red braces. His jet-black hair had been parted to the right and Brylcreemed flat to his scalp. 'What do you want?' he said.

Archie pointed to the front door, but the man shook his head. 'I'm not interested.'

'I'm not selling anything. Are you Arthur Lawton?'

'What's that to you?'

'I think I'm your son,' said Archie.

*

A coal fire crackled away in the grate.

Archie sat in silence at a pine dining table, trying to ignore the sickly smell of grease rising from a sink full of dirty pots.

A whistling kettle sounded on top of the stove. Arthur poured boiling water into a teapot, mashed the leaves with a spoon and put on the lid. 'Your mum died when you were a toddler,' he said, splashing sterilised milk, which Archie hated, into two mugs. He poured the tea, placed a mug in front of Archie and sat down in the chair opposite.

'My mum's alive and well,' said Archie. 'I've just left her at home.'

Arthur stood up. 'Why have you come here?'

'Tell me what happened,' said Archie.

'A bus hit her. Drunk driver–'

'–I mean between you and her.'

Arthur put his hands in his pockets and shrugged. 'It just happened. She worked for me, helped with my kiddies.'

'After your first wife died. Seems to be a bit of a habit with you. Dying wives. Why didn't you want me?'

'I think you should go.'

Archie cried.

'We couldn't have kept you,' said Arthur, sitting back down at the table. 'I already had seven kiddies to feed. She found you a good home.'

Archie pulled a handkerchief out of his trouser pocket, blew his nose and wiped his eyes. 'What was she like?'

'She was nice, kind,' said Arthur, leaning back in his chair.

'Did you love her?'

'Of course. We got married, didn't we?' Arthur faced the fire, crouched down, picked up an iron poker and prodded at the crackling coal. 'You should go home,' he said. 'You need to be with your family.'

*

He stared out of the kitchen window, thought about his dad growing the lawn from seed, chasing the birds off the freshly dug earth, beaming with joy when a blanket of lush green shoots emerged, edging the borders to show off his prize rhododendron bushes, treasuring the eucalyptus tree that always filled the summer air with a minty, menthol, honey scent.

His dad. He'd given him his car. AFD16OB, the wings full of fibreglass, the roof leaking when it rained. He'd pulled a favour with one of his old navy mates and sorted Archie an apprenticeship at Wellman Cranes. Archie wanted to be a binman. 'What a bloody ambition,' said his dad. He'd taken him for his first pint when he was sixteen because he didn't know how long he had left. 'He's all right,' he'd said to the barman, another ex-navy mate.

Archie walked through the porch, into the garden, reached the eucalyptus tree and kicked the gnarled trunk. Next door's tomcat meowed from the top of the tin fence, dropped down onto the lawn, strode over to the rhododendron bushes, lifted his back end and sprayed.

*

Archie stood behind the two-foot-high metal railings that circled the lake in Walsall Arboretum, thinking about his mate, Terry. As kids, they'd dared each other to swim out to the conifer-covered island. 'You could reach it,' said Terry. 'You're a better swimmer than me.'

'Yeah,' said Archie. 'But you're daft enough to try.'

He picked up his stone-filled rucksack, pushed his arms through the straps, fastened the belt across his stomach and stepped over the railings. He squelched off the bank, soaking his canvas baseball pumps and drenching his socks. He carried on walking, the ice temperature of the lake working its way over his ankles, over his knees, tugging at his thick denim Brutus jeans.

He waded, still staring at the island, thinking of nothing.

A shout.

Two men running towards his set-off point, their fishing rods rooted into the bank, floats bobbing the water in search of a bite.

They shouted again.

Archie quickened his pace, used his arms to push forward. The water lapped over his waist. His feet slipped on the bottom. He steadied himself, refocused on the island, moved forward again. Another step. The water up to his chest. And another, and another… the island shimmered out of view. A gasp. The lake stole his breath. Up again. Another gasp. He felt the pull of the rucksack dragging him down. 'Tommy,' he screamed. 'Tommy.'

He opened his mouth and forced the water into his lungs.

Darkness grabbed him.

*

The woman pulled out a packet of More menthol cigarettes and a silver flick lighter from her trouser pocket. She lit up, took a long draw and blew smoke towards the ceiling. She leaned forward in the chair, the cigarette held tightly between the index and middle finger of her right hand. 'It's over, Tommy. Time for Archie to move on.'

The image of his brother disappearing beneath the lake had been replaced on the plasma-filled wall with Archie standing at the side of the millpond, the woman watching him from the cast-iron bench. The wall zoomed in on Archie's face. The screen froze. 'That lake,' Tommy said. 'I was inside his head… he called my name.'

'He never wanted to hurt you,' said the woman.

'Why did Mum tell him?'

'She couldn't keep the secret any longer.'

Tommy turned out of bed, stood up and walked over to the wall. He traced a line around Archie's image, letting his touch come to rest on Archie's face. He felt the bubbling plasma pulsating beneath the tips of his fingers. 'I love him so much,' he said. 'I wish I could tell him.'

'He knows,' the woman said, walking over and putting her arm around his shoulder. She guided Tommy back to the bed. He lay down and she pulled the blanket up under his chin. 'Sleep well,' she whispered in his ear.

Tommy smiled and closed his eyes.

Blues and Twos

Tomo. A bullshitter with arrogance bursting out of every pore.

Me. A bag of nerves mummy's boy.

An odd couple, but we needed each other for a while.

Planning to kill him may have been an overreaction, but that's the way my head worked at the time.

*

We met at a police cadet interview.

He kept saying things like, "piece of piss" and "walk in the park", which infected me, made me feel taller, raised my expectations. 'We'll have a drink when this is done,' he said. 'Go and celebrate.'

I went in first. All I could focus on was the crown over the pip on the chief superintendent's epaulettes, signalling his anointed king status. 'We're going to take a chance on you,' he said. I nearly threw up over the desk.

'You okay?' said Tomo when I came out.

'Yeah,' I spluttered. 'They said yes.'

'Never in doubt,' he said.

*

Police cadet. Mum nearly burst when I told her. She had the adventure of a fully fledged sergeant and constable coming to her council estate flat as part of the pre-interview checks. 'Looks like his feet are big enough,' said the sergeant when he saw my Doc Martens in the hall.

Mum told this story over and over again for the rest of her life.

I cringed when she told me they'd been – the dog urine smell from our incontinent mongrel, the sandy-coloured hairs he left over the furniture. 'They must have needed a good wash and brush down after leaving here,' I said.

'They seemed happy enough to me,' said Mum and carried on washing up.

My girlfriend, Lorraine, made a banner with the film title *All Coppers Are...* substituting the word *"bastards"* with *"loveable"*, which impressed me no end because it had the same number of letters.

We'd been seeing each other for a few months before the cadet news, met at a local disco, me doing my usual watching the floor routine, her walking over and asking me to dance. I never found out why. Long auburn hair, athletic body, clever, smart. Any bloke in the room would have raced across the Sahara to dance with her.

She hated Tomo on sight. 'What a wanker,' she said.

Tomo made things worse when we double-dated a couple of times, both times with Lorraine's friends. The first girl, Dawn, told Lorraine he was obsessed with getting his hand inside her bra. 'You've got lovely tits,' he told her.

The second girl, Karen, told pretty much the same tale. ‘He put his hand up my skirt and asked what knickers I had on. I told him to piss off.’

Tomo told a different story. ‘Too desperate, mate. Gagging for it. I couldn’t be bothered.’

I finished up going to Baron’s Court nightclub with him on a Thursday night. The lads’ night out he called it. He had a regular girlfriend, Mandy, but that didn’t stop him picking up other women. I was his hanger-on, his “best pal”, but I finished up as counsellor for the girls he let down. I remember one girl, Maggie, a schoolteacher who made extra money working behind the bar of an evening. He’d seen her a few times and then dumped her. She used to drive me home at the end of the night, Tomo having long disappeared with his latest conquest. We sat in her Ford Capri outside my mum’s flat until four in the morning, her telling me how much she loved him. He laughed when I told him. ‘Her,’ he said. ‘She’s too old, and she howls like a dog when you give her one.’

I should have sprinted away, taken Lorraine’s advice, but being Tomo’s mate, one of his pals, made life easier. Being with him meant you were with the king of chat, the master storyteller, the shiniest boots on parade.

He bought me an access-to-all-areas pass, but it came at a price.

*

By the summer of 1979, the cracks showed.

I convinced Lorraine to give him another chance, and we went away on a camping weekend to Wales with him and Mandy, him in his Ford Cortina, me following in my Chrysler Avenger. He took off at speed down the narrow country lanes, overtaking everything in his path, leaving us stranded because he knew the way.

I tried to keep up, but my nerves and the speed of his car made that impossible.

With the help of an old map of my mum's, we pulled onto the campsite at 11pm.

He greeted us with a beaming smile. 'You took your time, mate,' he said.

'You really are a prat,' said Lorraine.

'What's the matter with you, darling?' said Tomo. 'Time of the month?'

I said nothing.

Lorraine dumped me when we got back home. 'You're like a puppet when he's around,' she said. 'We need a break.'

'You're best rid,' said Tomo when I told him. 'She's too mouthy that one.'

The next week on the parade ground, I was at the front of the squad, and I heard sniggering behind me. I looked around. Tomo was mimicking my rigid arm marching. Even the drill sergeant laughed. 'Sorry, mate,' said Tomo, holding up his hands. 'But you are putting us off.'

After that, it became open season. Everyone had permission to laugh at the stooge. Tomo led the banter. 'Bravo's having one of his dumb moods again,' he'd say if I was sitting in silence on the bus back home. They'd all turn and look.

The more they laughed, the more I retreated inside my head.

*

Elan Valley, the final cadet test.

A month camping in the dirty wet of Wales, sleeping on duckboards, living like hoboes. Squads of eight stinking, testosterone-inflated teenagers sharing a tent, united by a forced camaraderie to beat the crap out of the other squads. My idea of Dante's nine circles of hell, but Tomo's seventh heaven. We were put in the same squad, the group photo making us look like a gang of borstal boys on a community outing. 'You'll need to raise your game, mate,' said Tomo. 'I don't want you letting us down.'

On arrival at camp, one of the constables yelled at us to double time off the minibus, drop our bags and wade into the testicles-in-your-groin cold of the River Elan. I gritted my teeth, not wanting to look like a weak link. 'I bet you're shitting yourself,' said Tomo as we sat in the white foam water, the current hissing past us.

Camp day. The constant drip, drip, drip of Welsh drizzle, ubiquitous midges gorging at sweaty faces, festering boots forever glued to my feet, stinking orange cagoules, muscle-tightening, bone-grinding exhaustion from the dawn until dusk exercise. Up at five, after a damp, shivering night, preparing for tent inspection at 6.30am, lining up outside the tent, possessions laid out in front of us, the instructors walking the line, picking at every miniscule speck of dust, unbounded joy smeared across their faces – prison shakedown we called it. Breakfast over, we'd start the day – PT sessions, assault course, volleyball, football, canoeing, abseiling, everything quicker, faster, better, the group encouraged to turn on the runts of the litter. Four weeks of competitions. 'I'll be captain,' said Tomo. No one argued. 'And you'll be my gofer,' he said, putting his arm around me.

One day, one of the lads from another squad floundered at the back of the group on a cross-country run, desperately sucking at the mist to try and take in more oxygen. The instructor bellowed at the rest of us, 'If he doesn't move his fucking fat arse, you lot will be doing this again.' He encouraged us to chant, "fat boy, fat boy, fat boy" over and over, which, led by Tomo, we did.

In truth, most of my squad were like me. Immature boys, first time away from home, scared and vulnerable: Urmo – boasted about his Jim'll Fix it badge, awarded to him for picking up litter in his local village; Smally – drove a Triumph Herald convertible and wanted to be a chef; Hobbs – had bright ginger hair and was a big Led Zeppelin fan. He treated us to a 2am tent rendition of "Stairway to Heaven". We sat agog, fascinated that he knew all the words. Winter – a bad-boy reputation, which never really left him. He would go on to be jailed for growing and selling cannabis – a spare room cultivator they called him. Mush – acne face, O level king who made no secret of wanting to rise through the ranks. He ended up getting kicked out of the force for smashing up his room at Tally Ho after he caught his girlfriend in bed with one of the instructors. Hoops – a marijuana-addicted Genesis fan who cried when they made him have a buzz cut. He smelt of patchouli oil, which we all thought came from his skin. Deprived of his funny fags, he sought solace in Park Drive and philosophy. He finished up becoming a Buddhist and living on a retreat in Scotland. One night, neither of us able to sleep, me and Hoops sat by the River Elan. 'You shouldn't take Tomo seriously,' he said.

I shrugged and carried on throwing stones into the water.

No one wanted to be in that place.

We needed to be shown a way to survive, of getting through the trauma.

Captain Tomo stepped up.

He gave the squad a distraction, a way to deflect the attention from them.

He gave them me.

I became the butt of his jokes, the morale boosting, "at least you're not as bad as Bravo".

Being his whipping boy shadow seemed to be the only deal in town.

And then he went too far.

*

Duty day.

We worked in the kitchen preparing meals, washing the pots, cleaning the campsite, all under the supervision of a moustachioed, twinkly eyed sergeant who doubled up as a chef. He told us stories of cadets he'd come across and some of the pranks they'd had to endure. Like a cadet on a mortuary placement who'd been convinced by an attendant to lie down on a metal stretcher and be pushed inside the body fridge. The door closed; the cadet stared up at the dark; a hand suddenly landed on his stomach; and another attendant on the stretcher next to him said, 'Cold in here, isn't it?'

He'd tell these stories and then belly laugh whilst stirring his pot of the day. Nothing made him laugh more than his tale of the bromide tubs, which flavoured the supper cocoa and kept the cadets' libido flattened. 'The instructors don't know this,' said Chef, 'but I put it in their tea as well, including the bloody commandant.'

Chef gave me the job of preparing peppers. I didn't like to ask, but I hadn't come across peppers on my 1970's council estate, so I picked up the knife and peeled away at the skin. He came behind me, cuffed me lightly across the back of the head, took the knife and showed me what to do, creating a memory that stayed with me all of my life.

Mid-afternoon we had a break from kitchen duties, and I used the time to walk to the postbox at the top of the valley and post my letters home. I wrote to Mum, but I also wrote to Lorraine, even though she'd dumped me. One day, it was unusually sunny, and I walked back from the kitchen thinking everyone would be lying on the grass, but as I got closer to the tent, I couldn't see anyone, and then I heard laughter from inside and Tomo's voice. 'Don't worry about me, Mum. I'll be alright. Try and bring Lorraine down on open day. I really need to see her.' I felt my cheeks flush as I tore open the flap in the tent. They were all sat on their duckboards. Tomo waved my letter at me. 'You really are a mummy's boy,' he said.

I snatched the letter out of his hand and ran out of the tent, my stomach churning.

He caught up with me as I walked up the hill and put his arm around my shoulder. 'Sorry, mate,' he said.

'What have I ever done to you?' I said.

'Nothing,' he said, smiling. 'But I need a way of keeping them together. You'll be fine. I'll look after you.'

He grinned, waiting for me to say something.

My head clicked.

'Okay,' I said, smiling at him.

That evening I sat by myself on the bank of the River Elan, jotting down in my notebook the various ways of ending his life. I looked up at the cloudless sky, the full moon reflecting off the water, the absence of artificial light showing up a trillion stars and galaxies. They called that place the lake district of Wales, so using the natural elements for murder seemed to be favourite: pushing him off a mountain, drowning him, setting him on fire, staking him out in the bleakness of the valley, letting the drizzle and midges do their work.

I rejected them all.

It needed more than me to overpower him, and there was no way the others would sign up. I wondered if Chef might let me have something from the kitchen, perhaps the bromide, to poison him. I wasn't sure if you could die from an overdose of bromide.

As it turned out, I needn't have worried.

*

A fastest assault course time meant we were the lead squad by the end of the second week, drawing a reward of a Saturday night out in the village of Elan.

We washed up as best we could and – still wearing our boots, probably stinking like a pen full of pigs, with a curfew time of 10pm – we trooped off into the one-horse, one-pub town for a couple of beers. 'I'm going to get laid,' said Tomo. 'I've been chucking that bromide cocoa away for a week. I get hard if the wind changes direction.'

'There'll be no one worth having,' said Hoops. 'I think they're all still shagging sheep.'

'There's always a hook to hang your hat on,' said Tomo.

We reached the village and found the pub. Tobacco-stained flock wallpaper, two old men playing dominoes and a couple of blokes at the bar, about our age, wearing Motorhead T-shirts. They all stopped talking when we walked in. Tomo strode over to the bar and ordered eight pints. He turned and faced us as the barman pulled at the beer pump. 'It's early,' he said.

'Early for what?' said a girl's voice. She stood up behind the bar. Brown eyes, dark curly hair, a naturally tanned, make-up-free face, which was a little flushed.

'Where did you come from?' said Tomo.

'Just sorting me dad's stock out,' she said, nodding at the barman.

'We're the police,' said Tomo. 'Don't worry, darling. I've not come to arrest you.'

'That's a shame,' said the girl.

The barman slapped two beers on the soggy mat and carried on pulling the rest of the pints. Tomo and the girl smiled at each other. I looked over at the Motorhead blokes. One of them had picked up the payphone receiver.

*

Half an hour later, Urmo, Smally and Hobbs had set themselves up on the pool table; the other three had cadged some darts off the barman. I stood at the bar, watching the pub, which was filling up. Someone put The Tourists, "So Good To Be Back Home Again" on the jukebox; the two old men in the corner tapped their feet to the rhythm. Tomo perched himself on a stool at the end of the bar and talked in whispered tones to the girl, who told us her name was Stacey. Every so often she'd laugh and slap Tomo's arm.

'Looks like he's doing alright,' said Hoops, who joined me at the bar, three empty beer glasses in his hand.

'Not sure her dad's happy though,' I said.

The sound of motorbike engines made us look out at the car park.

Two Kawasaki bikes.

Their leather-clad riders dismounted and were met by the two Motorhead blokes, who'd left the pub and were waiting for them. The next thing we knew all four of them walked through the bar door.

'Come away, Stacey,' said the barman, grabbing his daughter's arm.

'Hey,' said Tomo, not looking round. 'We were talking.'

'Talking's over, mate,' said one of the bikers.

'And who might you be?' said Tomo, standing up and facing him.

'Her fiancé,' said the biker, pushing Tomo in the shoulder.

'Ex-fiancé,' said Stacey, pulling herself free from her dad's grip.

Urmo, Smally and Hobbs walked over from the pool table and joined us at the bar, Urmo and Hobbs still holding their pool cues. The other biker stepped forward, followed by the Motorhead blokes. The pub went graveyard quiet. Winter and Mush walked over and stood next to Tomo. The first biker looked at the barman, who shook his head.

Tomo smiled and held out his hand. 'Looks like you've been stood down, mate. No hard feelings.'

Stacey laughed.

The biker ignored Tomo's hand and leaned into his face. 'You'll keep,' he said. 'I'm not finished with you.'

Tomo turned and sat back down on the stool. Stacey kissed him on the cheek. 'My hero,' she said.

The bikers walked out of the pub, and everyone went back to their drinks.

The barman looked at the Motorhead blokes.

They nodded and followed the bikers.

I could see through the window they were all talking to each other in the car park.

*

We managed to get four pints in before Hobbs rounded us up to head back to camp. Tomo stayed stuck to his stool at the end of the bar, whispering to Stacey, the barman's face going redder and redder. 'You'd better drag him away,' said Hobbs.

I walked over and put my hand on Tomo's back. 'Time to go,' I said.

He winked at Stacey.

She blushed and walked along the corridor at the back of the bar.

Tomo watched her go. 'I've just got a bit of business, mate,' he said. 'You go. I'll see you later.'

'You're mad,' I said. 'You know they're waiting for you. And what about the curfew?'

'I'll get back into the camp,' he said. 'And you lot can cover for me. Anyway, the way I'm feeling, it won't take long.'

'And what about the bikers? If they catch you on your own.'

'You worry too much,' he said. 'She's taking me to her auntie's shed. By the time they think of that, I'll be back on that duckboard.'

I looked across at the Motorhead blokes. 'At least walk out with us,' I said.

He drained his beer. 'Probably best,' he said. 'We don't want Daddy getting suspicious. She's meeting me up the lane.'

The eight of us strode out of the pub together. I could feel eyes boring into the back of my neck. 'Jesus,' said Hoops when we got outside. 'I'll not miss that place.'

'Time for me to love and leave you guys,' said Tomo.

Hobbs laughed. 'You're not…'

'Don't bother,' said Hoops. 'I can tell by his face his dick's in charge.'

Tomo headed right out the car park and scuttled off down the lane.

We went left and back along the narrow track to camp.

*

We trekked through the drizzle in a line, tight against the hedge, past the reservoir, towards the rickety iron bridge which crossed the River Elan. Hobbs led the way, me at the back.

My head clicked.

I stopped walking. 'I'll catch you up,' I said. 'I've left my gloves in the pub.'

They all faced me.

'I'll come back with you,' said Hoops, who was directly in front of me.

'I'll be okay,' I said.

'You sure?' said Hobbs. 'Those guys meant business.'

'They're not after me,' I said. 'You go. I'll run there and back and catch you up before camp.'

'You might be coming back with Tomo,' said Hoops. 'He looked like he was in a hurry.'

I walked into the pub car park and saw the Motorhead blokes standing over by the bins, the glow from their cigarettes showing them up in the dark. 'Hey, you,' one of them shouted and they both walked over to me.

I stood perfectly still and waited for them to reach me. The bloke who'd shouted, the bigger of the two, pushed me in the chest. 'Where's your mate?' he said. 'That's our sister he's gone off with.'

'That's what I've come back for,' I said.

'What do you mean?' he said, pushing me in the chest again.

'Your auntie's shed. I'm assuming you know about it.'

'Why would you–'

'He's a prick,' I said.

'I'll phone the others,' said the smaller one, walking off towards the pub.

'He mustn't know I told you,' I said.

The bloke took a drag on his fag and grinned. 'Don't worry, mate. By the time we've finished with him it won't matter who told us.'

I made it back to camp before curfew. The others were already tucked up in their sleeping bags, trying to get comfortable on the duckboards. 'No sign of Tomo,' said Hobbs as I walked into the tent.

'No,' I said.

'Must have taken longer than he thought,' said Mush.

'Yeah,' I said. 'It must have.'

Neighbourhood Watch

6am.

From my house on a hill at the end of a cul-de-sac, I watch the street waking up. A mist sticks to the air like superglue. I prefer the big arrival mornings, when a fireball sun creeps over the horizon and bursts through to banish the night.

My sentry post is a wicker chair set slightly back from the bay window. I partially draw the vertical blinds and position a pot of freshly brewed Jamaican Blue and a jug of hot milk on my glass-top coffee table. I pour the coffee into my Jamie Oliver mug. The mug has a slogan on its side: "get your coat" and on the bottom, "you've pulled". I worry about how much it makes me smile. Paul Simon's greatest hits CD is playing at a low hum through my Denon music system.

I wish I could sleep better, but then I would miss the awakening.

Paul opens up with "Lincoln Duncan", telling me about the couple in the next room. I wonder who they are, what they did with their lives, whether or not they won their prize.

I sit down and open my notebook.

Here comes Dumpy, the redhead with her two British bulldogs yanking at their leads, drool streaming from their sloppy mouths. She's on her own now. Most people seem to be on their own these days. I wonder when that became a thing. Her husband left her and the dogs a couple of years ago, ran off with a woman who worked on the bacon counter at Lidl. A tart, Dumpy calls her. The dogs speed up a bit as their home comes into view. Dumpy speeds up as well, but she trips in her sloppy slippers, nearly goes to ground, just about saves herself with her one hand. The dogs stop, turn and look at her while she brushes down her Superwoman onesie. She pulls the bulldogs back towards her and carries on walking down her path.

A stranger sits on the bench by the oak tree, his legs crossed and arms folded.

He's watching the house.

I should go and ask him what he's doing, but that would interrupt my surveillance.

He uncrosses his legs, reaches into his pocket, pulls out a phone, taps away for a few seconds and then puts the phone back in his coat.

Mr Lorry Driver walks down his path. He gets into his BMW, off to pick up his cab. He'll be away for a few days, but, within half an hour of him pulling off his drive, Grey Beard, his best mate, will turn up in a Mini Metro, go into the house, and I'll hear creaking bed springs, a rattling headboard and groans of "yes, yes, yes" from Mrs Lorry Driver. When her husband returns, Grey Beard will turn up again, this time with his partner, an older woman who wears gold bracelets on each wrist and hooped earrings.

The two couples will sit in the back garden, laughing and drinking beer.

I make a note and then look back towards the oak tree.

*

The only other heartbeat in my house is Tai, my little black, twenty-year-old she-cat who wandered in as a six-week-old stray on Bonfire Night, her kitten pads bleeding, her head bouncing in terror at every firework, daring me to put her back in the icy warzone.

Tai is now my longest relationship in my adult life. She sits with me in these early morning vigils, staring through the blind slats, yawning, looking up every so often to check all is okay with the world.

Another front door opens. Number fourteen. Anthony and Cleopatra off to work in their separate Minis. Cleopatra attends the village hairdresser twice a week, her nails a work of art, filed, shaped, painted to perfection. Anthony spends most of his home time outside in his muddy blue overalls, cutting the grass, weeding, digging the borders, smoking his cigarettes at the top of the drive, barred from the house. Cleopatra makes him sit on The Guardian when he goes indoors for meals. They dote on their daughter, Chardonnay, an only child, and obsess about their rabbit, which regularly escapes through the fence. Cleopatra knocks on neighbours' doors, imploring them to search their bushes, shouting Mopsy at the top of her voice. The bunny is always found, usually chewing on a dandelion leaf, with a guilty look and twitching nostrils.

The man on the bench stands up, straightens his cap and walks up the street.

Panic rises in my stomach. He walks past and out of the cul-de-sac to a red Volkswagen Beetle parked on the main road. I strain my neck to see what he's doing. He opens the back door, grabs a thermos flask off the back seat and walks back to the bench. He sits down, opens the flask, fills the plastic cup, the steam from the liquid merging with the early morning mist. He takes a sip and looks again at my house.

I fear he can see me. The blinds are partially drawn and I'm sitting away from the window, but I push my chair back further and pull the coffee table towards me. My paranoia bubbles to the surface. Everyone looking, pointing, laughing, looming. The man throws the dregs from his cup under the oak tree and crosses his legs again. A pinstriped suit and navy-blue tie underneath his raincoat. He's wearing black Chelsea boots.

I write it all down.

A noise. A window opening. Number ten, the neighbouring house on the other side of me. The brothers are getting up. Sounds of their life through paper-thin walls. The older one, a chef, shouts every night, 'I'm off down the Nags,' before driving his battered white transit van to the pub, back at midnight, parking it diagonally, two feet away from the kerb, going into the house, slamming the front door, pissing a waterfall into the toilet.

Tai meows. She wants her breakfast.

The man on the bench lights a cigarette and takes a drag. He blows smoke towards the oak tree.

Tai meows again, a little louder this time.

*

I sit back in my chair and refill my coffee mug.

Tai crunches away at her biscuits. She likes to eat these next to me in the lounge, afraid of missing something or, more likely, just wanting the company. I realise that I'm her world, the only other sentient being she meets.

Number fifteen opens his door. Stumpy Short-Arse. He used to live with Six-Foot Blondie. Every Sunday in the summer, she would clean her BMW sports car wearing a bosom-squeezing, white cotton T-shirt and buttock-revealing, frayed denim shorts. Her ex-husband, also blond, also six foot, visited the house she shared with Stumpy. One day, Stumpy fell off his motorbike at the end of the cul-de-sac and ex-husband helped him limp down the drive, one gentle step at a time, Blondie watching from the back gate, pissing herself. Stumpy lives on his own now. Superintendent, his neighbour, says he can hear him through the walls talking to his budgie. 'Just you and me now, mate.'

Superintendent opens his door, number seventeen, and walks out with his lurcher on a lead, heading off for their early morning walk. I like the comfort Superintendent brings to the street. Nothing moves without him popping up like a meercat on prairie surveillance. He does his rounds of the neighbours several times a day, picking up the local gossip, checking out what's new in everyone's life, sharing his latest doctrines on the state of the economy or the NHS. He had triple heart bypass surgery a few years ago, said it felt like he'd been hit by a train, recovered by sitting on a deck chair in his front garden, keeping an eye on his world. His wife rarely appears in public, goes away on holiday alone with the kids. Superintendent says he'd rather stay at home. He doesn't trust all those foreigners. His kids used to play chicken up my drive, ringing my doorbell, running away. I heard them call me a miserable old bastard one Halloween, when I didn't open the door for trick or treat. They've grown out of that now.

Tai finishes her biscuits and wanders off into the kitchen.

She scrapes away in the litter tray.

There's a gush of urine as she empties her bladder.

*

I joined Prozac nation in the 1990s, trying to dampen my thoughts. I'd twisted myself into a catatonic state, never speaking when socialising, frightened to death of giving anything away or saying something stupid. If I did utter a word, it would be in hushed tones, which I heard in my head as me shouting, trying to get everyone's attention. The Prozac brought me out of the shadows, hard-copied my invisibility cloak, but a chemically coshed Jiminy Cricket still lurks across my synapses, ready to hit the flight or fight button at a nanosecond's notice.

The man on the bench puts out his cigarette. A debt collector. Someone has taken out a loan on my house, defaulted on the payments and now the bailiffs have come to collect. Or perhaps he's working for my daughter, my lost blood, searching for her inheritance. An image fills my head. Five years old, snotty nose, dirty dress, sitting in the gutter outside her nan's house. I'd spent most of the '90s in therapy, trying to assuage the guilt. Jungian collective unconscious, Rogers' self-actualisation, Freud's libido. All useless. I still cry at night. She'd be thirty-five now. The end of my gene pool.

Beads of sweat pop on my forehead; my pulse rate ratchets up through the gears, trying to force its way out of my chest, competing with the chemical stupor imposed by the drugs.

I take a deep breath and wipe my face with my hand.

Paul meets his old lover, fears he's going to do some damage as he watches the cars through his window. "Still Crazy After All These Years".

Flip-Flop opens his curtains; dirty grey nets shift in the corner as he sneaks a look at the world. He lives with his daughter, who spends most of her life smoking weed in Flip-Flop's shed. I don't mind. I suck in the smell as it drifts over the fence into my garden.

The man on the bench lights another cigarette.

*

It's getting light. I move my chair further back from the window, which restricts my view of the oak tree and the man. I stand up and lean my head around. Tai stands up as well. She stretches out her old bones, sits down and waits for whatever we're going to do next.

The man on the bench stands up.

He might not be watching my house; my crazy head might be deluding me, setting me off down a dead-end street. Seven-year-old me believed my life was a game show, broadcast by the gods as live entertainment, controlled by an audience who could press fate buttons to set challenges and decide my destiny. Dr Dwyer said I had an overactive imagination and I would grow out of it.

I push the thought away.

The man is definitely staring at my window.

A car turns into the cul-de-sac, a diesel engine, a black cab. It pulls up in front of the man. A woman wearing a red beret gets out the back, pays the driver and turns to face the man. They shake hands. The woman is holding a red A4 folder. She opens it and the man looks inside. The cab drives out of the street. The man throws away his cigarette and points towards my house. They stand there looking.

I step back further into the lounge. Tai presses her nose through the blind slats and against the window, picking up on my anxiety, sensing something might be happening. She looks back at me. There's a smudge where her nose has touched the glass.

A van pulls up outside Superintendent's. Patel Builders emblazoned on the side. They're quite famous locally for their advertising slogan, "you've tried the cowboys, now give the Indians a go". Superintendent does some cash-in-hand work for them, mainly laying block paving. He shouldn't be doing it, not with his heart.

I haven't seen them pick him up for a few months.

I reach for my notebook.

My doorbell rings. Tai looks up at me.

*

Paul greets the darkness as an old friend. "The Sound of Silence".

I used to hide under the duvet as a child, creating imaginary worlds.

I pick up the Denon remote control and turn up the volume.

Mum and Dad. I hate talking about them. It always makes people say sad things about their mum and dad. I should talk about them more, dredge it up out of my guts, slap it on the kitchen table, give the therapists something visceral to hear. I wrote it all down years ago. Better out than in. I'll read it to them. Give them the full story. Perhaps then they'll understand.

My doorbell rings again.

I can see them through the blind slats. The man and Beret Woman. 'Mr Jackson,' says the man. 'Local council. Neighbourhood office. We've had complaints.'

'He won't answer,' I hear Stumpy say.

'No,' says Superintendent, his lurcher at his feet. 'He just sits in there all day watching. Thinks we can't see him writing it all down in his notebook.'

I look up the street. Flip-Flop leans on his bin, grinning like a Cheshire cat; Anthony and Cleopatra stand by their Minis, looking like chauffeurs waiting for their passengers to return from the pub; Mrs Lorry Driver stands on her doorstep, straight from the shower, wearing a white bath towel wrapped around her body; Dumpy opens her front door, slow on the uptake, nearly too late for the party, still wearing her sloppy slippers; Stumpy and Superintendent stand at the top of my drive, arms folded, florid faces.

I wonder which one of them has reported me.

I'll make a note just in case I need it.

'Can't you do something?' says Stumpy.

I jump as the man places a warrant card against my window. 'Let us in, Mr Jackson. We need to talk.'

I try to read the name on the card, but I'm too far away and it's partially obscured by one of the blind slats. It ends in ski. Russian.

I close the blinds, look at Tai and put my finger to my lips.

She meows, places her head on her paws and stares up at me through cataract-covered eyes.

A Day in the Life of a Head Fairy

Him.

Let me tell you the rules. I'm guessing you were expecting a woman, white tutu dress, silver crown, glittery wand, but that's not how this works. It's all sex neutral when you die. You see, there are three routes out of limbo: heaven, for the goody two shoes; hell, for the stains and – here's where it gets complicated – a middle-rider, second-chancer option, for those who've fractured a few laws. That's me. We get to be head fairies, to come back and guide a living host. If we do well, paradise awaits; if we don't, it's the fire pit for all eternity.

Makes me shudder when I think about it, but at least I get another go.

Not everyone gets a fairy. You have to be a good subject, responsive to guidance and, most importantly, vulnerable. And fairies can't just do what they want. They, the bosses, tell you what you are, how you're meant to behave.

I'm a strive-for-less guide, a restrictor.

I'll show you.

Look. My host's over there on the phone. He's not a pretty sight. Trust me to get a sucker. I've had to check a couple of times to see if he's got prat tattooed on his forehead. Every week she whistles, and he goes running. She'll want a lift back from the nightclub, want him parked up outside, panting like a faithful hound. And then he'll drive to their country lane, get in the back of the car and claim his kiss and fumble reward. His candy time. I'm serious. That's what he calls it. Give me a second. I just need to whisper a couple of one-liners.

Tell her you're busy… get a life… hang up.

He never listens, but I can't ignore it. It's not all tinsel and wings in this job. They like you to earn your keep. Hang on a minute. He's by the mirror now, putting on his designer suit and a splash of Kouros. I'll give him a few more prods.

Stick your jeans and sweatshirt on… she won't care as long as you've got the car… you're already on a promise.

That last one made him think. I might use that again. This fairy game's all a bit trial and error, and I'm still on probation. Fair enough. We've all got to start somewhere, and it's not as though there's a rule book. It depends on your host, and my man's riddled with love. It's nice and cosy for a while until the deadliest virus known to the human race turns on you. And that's when you need me. The restrictor. It's not easy. The only weapon they've given me is a few seed-of-doubt bombs. You know the sort of thing: The what-ifs? The what-abouts? It's all garbage, but it's amazing what happens when those marbles get rolling inside your head. We're off now. See you in a bit.

*

Look. I'm down here on the driver's seat. It's all getting a bit grunt, grind and groan back there. I had to get out of his head for a break. I bet you're wondering why the back of a car. Simple answer, they still live with their parents. Kids, just turned eighteen. Young love, the most virulent strain of the disease. Mind you, sometimes it gets worse with age.

Something different happened tonight. We pulled up outside the club, they did their usual kiss and reach-for-the-bucket hello; I settled back and waited for him to pull away, but she reached across and put her hand on his knee. 'There's something I need to tell you,' she said.

Well, that woke me up. The big kiss-off. I whispered a she's dumping you message for good measure. But this is what she said: 'I want you to come with me to the club. I want us to be a proper couple.'

Now, don't judge me, but I might have given you the wrong impression. You see, my man's not exactly Mr Sociable. He goes through the motions, offers to do lots of things, but he doesn't expect her to say yes. I'd have bet my pension he wouldn't agree, but then, and this is really irritating, he smiled his bubblegum smile, the one that always disengages his brain, and said, 'I'll try. I miss you.'

She threw her arms around his neck and kissed him.

I pitched a what are you doing? at him, but, to be honest, my heart wasn't in it, and it was pretty obvious I couldn't compete with her strawberry lip gloss and white musk perfume. I'll have to bide my time, wait until he's in the club, wait until he's doing his gangly dancing… oh, my God, there's a girl sitting in the passenger seat. Dewy, almond eyes. 'Who are you?'

'I'm Becky, madam's head fairy.'

She's looking up at me, her red hair cascading down her back. This isn't fair. I'm over all that. I'll take a deep breath, try to dampen down the hammer of my pulse. Can you hear it? I'm sure she can hear it. Did I tell you about her eyes?

*

Her.

I'm probably much more to your expectation. Well, at least I'm a woman. But I'm not Tinker Bell, which is why I'm doing this job. Mr Fairy seems to like the name Becky. Whatever gets him through the night, I guess. I notice he hasn't told me his name. That's good. He's probably a Nigel or, even worse, Dave. I'll call him something Italian. Roberto. Yes, that'll do. Nice and slippery, rolls around your mouth. Roberto.

I'm looking up at him, trying to make the best use of my time outside madam's head. He's got his mouth open. That'll be my red hair. Always makes them salivate. He's not meant to leave his host, but I'm one to talk. Mine's on the back seat with Eeyore. I keep waiting for him to do his Hitchhiker's robot impression. You know the one: "Life. Don't talk to me be about life". He's kind enough, but I don't think many brain cells come into it. And he's not exactly classy. I mean, the rear of an Avenger down a country lane. It wouldn't do for me. Four stars, a wine waiter and then they might, just might, have reached first base. Not this chap. He's currently got my princess trying to work out how to get her legs comfortable. It's not easy, the headrests, the gearstick, the handbrake. I've told her, stick your legs out the window, but she's a bit too prim and proper for that. I shouldn't knock him really, but, as I keep telling her, you're Maradona and he's Vinnie Jones. Shouldn't even be on the same pitch. I do my best to put her in the shop window, get her dancing in the strobe light to Roxy Music's, "Dance Away", whispering, look at all those cuties drooling over you. Careful, you might trip over their tongues.

She never sees them, dances with her eyes closed, sees Eeyore inside her head, wishes he was there. He's never coming, I whisper. And he wouldn't be dancing if he did.

Every night she calls him, and he always turns up. I mean, come on, that says it all. A click of her fingers and he races out in the middle of the night with his Barbra Streisand Guilty tape.

Anyway, I have to confess, they seem to hit each other's buttons. Ding. Dong. His orgasms make me laugh. That little whimper just before. You can set your clock to it. If you think about it, sex is a funny thing. The bits of our body that matter most in the act are pretty ugly when you look at them in the cold light of day. I guess that's why we cover them up under layers. But wham, when the juices start flowing, or lovemaking as princess calls it, getting at Elephant Man's appendages is pretty frenetic.

My host is a romantic, claims she can't have it without feeling something. Losing her virginity. Now that became drama special with extended highlights. Karen, her best mate, lost hers on Grimsby Town football pitch. The bloke, Tim, a big fan, told his mates he'd scored on the penalty spot. Karen said it was more like the halfway line, and they didn't need extra time. That wasn't going to happen to my host. Scented candles, Egyptian cotton sheets covered in French perfume, Rock Hudson and Doris Day running hand in hand across a white sand beach, the camera panning away as they kissed, foamy waves crashing against shoreline rocks.

I told her it was pie in the sky and, as usual, I was right.

Mickey Kumar snatched her cherry in Mac Fisheries' car park in the passenger seat of his TR7. A Hindu, born in India, raised in Bilston, his mum came from Begur village on the outskirts of Bangalore. One of my host's mates, Beth, sang Joe Jackson's, "Is She Really Going Out with Him?" whenever she walked past. My host told her to piss off, which would have been my advice, but she beat me to it.

Mickey dumped her the day after the Mac Fisheries fumble. 'So you've had your fun and now you're running,' she said.

'Lighten up,' he said. 'Mum and Dad want me to marry a nice Indian girl. They've already sorted a list of possibilities.'

'A list?'

'Yeah, that's the way we do things. It's better than meeting some random girl in a bar.'

Not lovemaking. Not Rock Hudson. A waste of space nobody's shag. That's reality.

The last we heard of Mickey, he'd married a white British Airways hostess from Milton Keynes. He met her in a nightclub.

Eeyore's fairy is cute. It's a pity we're not allowed. He should know that, but it's not stopping him having a good look. They don't like us getting up close and personal, something to do with karma. We have to repent, repent, repent, make up for our misdemeanours in former lives. Boring. Boring. Boring. Seriously, I'd better behave. It's a good gig, and the alternative doesn't bear thinking about. Still, a bat of the eyelids, letting the skirt slide up my thigh.

Okay, he's gone, jumped back into his host's head.

I might have broken him, sent him into hiding.

It's good timing really. It sounds like they're done in the back seat. We're in holding after stage now. To be fair, he's pretty obliging. The difficulty is knowing for how long. It gets cold in this car without the engine running, and she's not dressed for that weather, her big tights and woolly jumpers not exactly conducive to flowing juices. One thing that didn't work was that spray she used to wear. I mean, who wants people shouting, 'I can smell your Charlie.' I put her right on that one.

All that talk of virginity has set me off. My first time. The rhythm method. He should have pulled out, but he stayed in. Six weeks later the indicator turned blue. But I mustn't think about that. It's ancient history. They're moving now. I'd better get back. You never know what she might say without me there. See you later.

*

Him.

He's in bed, his snore, snore, snore, puff, puff, puffing away to the ceiling. I had to listen to Phil Collins, "Hello, I Must Be Going" all the way home, my host singing every word. I kept telling him, it's Phil we want to hear, not you. I might as well talk to myself, which, most of the time, I am. Part of my probation is a test to see if I can handle a numbskull. Trust me. I can see the signal connections in his brain, and there's barely a glimmer.

He's head obsessed, that's the problem, spends most of his time locked-in, blaming himself for the world, full of self-loathing. He should stay on his own, write his stories, create his imaginary worlds. Anything solitary. That's when he excels. I caught him last week talking to posters of famous film stars in the café he goes to in Ironbridge. Marilyn Monroe, James Dean, Audrey Hepburn. Luckily, they're in the toilet so no one saw him, but, well, it's all a bit sad. I told him. They're not real. Get a proper friend.

It seemed to pull him to his senses, but, my God, he is a proper Horace Wimp.

I'm glad tonight's over if I'm honest. Becky. Now she's a curveball. I've never met another head fairy, not in the flesh. We're all neutralised when they bring us in for reprogramming. You can't tell who's who or what's what. But Becky was naked. Not in the sense of no clothes, that would have made me burst, but she wasn't camouflaged. I could see, well, that flash of thigh. It reminded me of… no, I mustn't. They'll be listening. It's bad enough we've exposed ourselves. There'll be repercussions.

I need to get my mind back on the job.

Work. I mean work.

Tonight. He's serious about the nightclub, about dancing. I could see from the way bits of his brain pinged when she asked him. The pleasure dome. He seems to hit that a lot when he's with her, but something changed in his head. He's trying to restructure, to work out how to impress her. I should be protecting him, keeping him safe. That's the point of me.

But that would mean losing Becky.

Stop thinking about her. That part of your life is over. You can never go back there. I wonder what Miss Pick-Me-Up-From-The-Nightclub is thinking. Hang on a minute, he's turning over. At least his snoring's stopped, but, oh, there it is, the farting anus. Thank God I'm in his head and not on the outside waiting for that smell to hit my nostrils. I mean, she can't really like him. I'd talk to him now, but his brain's in slumber mode. There's not a lot of point being a head fairy when the head's asleep. Not that they let us nod off. We have to stay vigilant, ever-ready.

Becky. Oh God, I'm thinking about her again. Well, that's not my fault. I have to think about something. I wonder what she made of me disappearing. He's rolling over, back on his back. And, there it is, the return of the snoring. I wish he'd make up his mind. It's like being in a washing machine every time he shifts. Perhaps I can see her again. If she makes a habit of popping out of her host's head and I do the same, we're bound to bump into each other. They can't blame us for accidents. I'll rest my eyes for a bit and give that some thought. I need all my energy to keep this big lump on the straight and narrow.

Ah, red hair, dewy eyes, bare thighs…

*

Her.

We're back home. Madam's in bed, naked, lightly perspiring, purring gently in her magic carpet dreams.

She's had her glass of hot milk, which is a must after the club. Her head tells me she's happy, but I'm a strive-for-more fairy, a never-settle-for-the-first-sweetie-you-see-in-the-shop sort of girl. Eeyore's fairy suits him. Looks a bit like him with his long, horse face and dopey expression. A bit like a basset hound. Perhaps it's true that dogs come to resemble their owners. I wouldn't mind looking like madam. We'd be poodles, lots and lots of powdering and pampering. Perfect.

My princess. Now she's definitely a high-maintenance girl, which suits me fine. There's a list of things she wouldn't be seen dead in – hooped earrings, short skirts, low-cut tops, anything Burberry, Jimmy Choo shoes. It's common sense really. I whisper it to her all the time – be a grown-up. Stay away from chav city. And that's another reason Eeyore's out of his depth. I mean, loving my sweetie is a man's job, and he's still riding his way through life on stabilisers.

Dead. We're the lucky ones. Middle Riders. Our karma doesn't allow us to move on, but we get to be carers for a living pod. It's a cool gig really, better than the sub-class who have no redemption, but, my God, it's frustrating as hell when your host doesn't play the game. I miss living. The thrill of the chase. Blink and you're heading for the light before you get a chance to make amends. I spent years in limbo before they decided what to do with me. Perhaps they'll give me another go if I get this assignment nailed… hang on. He's arrived in her head now. They're swimming in the Indian ocean, azure sea, bath temperature lagoon, a pod of dolphins at their side. Please. He's a council-estate kid. Wake up. He's never going to earn enough. It's not a Spandau Ballet video.

It's no good. They're still swimming. I'm in a bit of a quandary really. I should be keeping my princess on the straight and narrow, reminding her of all the George Michaels left in the world, but that cute fairy, well, if I'm honest, he's set my juices gushing a bit, and it's been a while. They'll know that, the bosses. I'll already be on the naughty step for not covering up in front of him. Live in the moment. Isn't that what they say? Maybe that doesn't apply to a penitent fairy. I'm not sure that's what I am. What's the point if we can't push a button every now and then?

My cutie. Roberto. He disappeared at Linford Christie speed. I wonder if he's one of those rule-stickler fairies. Not from the expression on his face when he saw my red hair. Anyway, I've always loved a fighter. It makes it more interesting when they wriggle. Next time madam's sorting her legs in the back of Eeyore's Avenger, me and cutie can ride it out in the front seat.

Now there's a dream.

Mim

July 1984.

An underpass gauntlet of snot-encrusted glue sniffers is part of my walk to the station.

I make it through, leaving me with two minutes before my train leaves.

Down the steps.

Platform 2B.

Slow down. Don't trip. Don't fall.

Tears pool in my lower lids. I blink them away, try to control my breathing, think about Jonesy and his skunks. They'll be back tomorrow.

And the next day.

And the day after that.

I emerge into a bustle world of tracks and tunnels. Diesel pings my nostrils. A whistle sounds. I run along the platform and jump on the end carriage of the ten-past-six train from Birmingham New Street to Walsall. I need to think, get my mind under control, try to work out a survival plan.

Three compartments along, a woman wearing a black beret and red pixie boots has her feet on a vacant seat. She's pulled the beret over her eyes.

I throw my bag into the overhead storage and cough. 'Excuse me,' I say.

She lifts the beret and looks me up and down. She's wearing a burgundy tartan wool trouser suit, which, with the beret and boots, isn't something I've seen before in the Black Country. I wonder if she's foreign, maybe Italian. 'I'd like to sit down,' I say.

'I'm terribly sorry,' she says, sitting up and shuffling back in her seat. 'I must have dozed off.'

'These things always send me to sleep as well,' I say, sitting down.

'Yes,' she says. 'That de-dum, de-dum, de-dum, de-dum noise ricochets in your head if you're not careful.'

I open my Guardian newspaper.

The train pulls away from the platform.

'Miriam,' she says. 'But most people call me Mim.'

'Steve,' I say. 'Nice to meet you, Mim.'

I go back to my paper, needing the distraction, trying to take my head to a different place. The miner's strike. A two-page interview with Arthur Scargill who claims Thatcher's government are tapping the phones of union leaders. Norman Tebbit dismisses it all as paranoia.

'You're a policeman,' says Mim.

I lower the broadsheet. 'How did you–'

'The boots, the clip-on tie, the civvy jacket.'

'Right,' I say, folding my paper and pulling my corduroy coat a little tighter. 'It's a bit of a giveaway I suppose.'

'You need my help,' she says, leaning forward and taking my hand.

My head clicks as soon as she touches me, and everything drops into slow motion. The train jerks along, still-frame by still-frame, the time-drag making my brain ultra-aware of the speed. Wheels bounce beneath me, clinging to the tracks, telegraph poles whizz past, slide by slide by slide. My sinuses block as the blood rushes to my extremities. Fight, flight, fight, flight. Too fast. We're going too fast. My Hornby set derailed if I turned the dial above two. Tighten stomach, clench buttocks, wait for the moment. I imagine the carriage sliding down the bank towards the canal, rolling over and over, the water looming, me crashing about, screaming, the splash.

'Stay with me,' says Mim. 'I can help you, but you have to tell me the full story.'

*

Mim listens in silence, the story falling out of my mouth like a tumour, the relief of telling someone washing over me, warming me from the inside out.

I force myself to stop talking.

'Are you okay?' she says.

I nod.

She reaches into a tartan carpet bag at her feet and pulls out a white, crisp cotton handkerchief. She hands it to me. I wipe the sweat, snot and tears from my face. 'Thank you,' I say, holding the handkerchief back towards her.

'Keep it,' she says. 'I have plenty.'

I blow my nose, take a deep breath and fill my lungs with the aroma of eucalyptus oil. Vicks. Mum smeared it on my chest as a child whenever a cold invaded my body. I hadn't used it for years.

'What are you going to do?' says Mim, patting my knee.

I look out of the window. A barley field, golden husks rhythmically swaying like the pendulum on a grandfather clock. I feel my eyes closing and rub my face, forcing myself to stay awake. 'Why have we stopped?' I say.

'Are they there every night?' she says, ignoring my question.

The image of the carriage rolling down the hill drops back into my head. Thank God we've stopped. Something isn't right. Perhaps they're inspecting the track, making it safe before we get going again. Be careful. Please be careful.

'Every night,' I say. 'All four of them sit on top of the underpass and gob on me as I walk through.'

'Why not go another way?'

She asks the right questions. Give her the answers. Help her. 'There is no other way out of the bus station. And they always run to the exit, catch me on the other side.'

I close my eyes. Blurting this out to a stranger on a train. I should report it, but I'd be the butt end joke of a laughing shift. Run, run, run, coward. Perhaps if I rest, give them a chance to save the train, help me avoid a crash.

I need to sleep, recharge my batteries.

Dropping down, down, down.

The train starts moving again.

De-dum, de-dum. De-dum, de-dum.

*

A clear blue sky, the sun stinging my eyes, the gob of the skinheads drying in my hair.

I make it through the underpass, but they circle me in front of a graffiti-covered wall. Someone has sprayed "Lozza Luvs Dave 4 Eva" in two-foot-high black paint letters. I push my hands in my trouser pockets to hide the shaking. 'What do you want?' I say.

Jonesy, the one with the Union Jack tattoo across his forehead, sniffs me up and down. The other three stand watching him, laughing and patting each other on the back.

I step backwards, but Jonesy pushes his face into mine, nose to nose. His breath stinks of stale life, as though some organism has set up home in his gums and died there a long time ago. He looks at me with big wide eyes, crusts of dried glue stuck to his unshaven chin, yellow-coated teeth that look like they need to be chipped not brushed. 'I can smell pig,' he says. 'Are you a piggy man, copper?'

I say nothing, afraid of the quiver that I know will sound in my voice. She'll come. I can feel her squeezing my hand. A screech. We all look up. Six crows perch on the subway wall, looking down on us.

Jonesy turns back to me and snorts a single sniff.

'He's a pig alright,' says one of the others. 'He stinks. I can smell him from here.'

They walk around, barging into me, shoving me backwards and forwards. 'Pig, pig; pig.'

'Oink, oink, oink.'

'Pig, pig; pig…'

'Gentlemen, gentlemen. This is no way to behave.'

They stop in unison and face the exit to the underpass.

Mim strides into view, Chris Eubank style. She's wearing a pinstriped suit, red pixie boots and carrying a blue leather attaché case with a crown and sceptre insignia embossed on the lid. There's an earpiece fixed into her left ear, a connecting wire running inside her jacket. She puts her mouth next to the lapel. 'Can you confirm everyone is in position, sir?'

'Who the fuck are you?' says Jonesy.

'I must caution you, young man,' says Mim, 'to choose your words very carefully. Everything here is being recorded.'

'Record that,' says the skinhead, putting up two fingers.

'Very droll,' says Mim, reaching into her jacket pocket. She pulls out a black wallet and flips it open under Jonesy's nose. 'MI5,' she says. 'I'm assuming you can read.'

Jonesy looks at the others and then at the wallet. He shrugs. 'What the fuck you want with us?'

'To get down to business,' says Mim. 'I understand you're the leader of this gang.' She waves a hand in the direction of the other three.

Jonesy shrugs again.

'Good,' says Mim. 'You seem to have a grievance with this officer.' She pushes the wallet back inside her jacket, kneels down and opens the attaché case. Two duelling pistols sit on a red velvet base. 'You can take your pick. They're both loaded with a single shot.'

'Hang on,' says Jonesy. 'Guns? We're just having a laugh.'

'Constable Shaw,' says Mim, handing me a pair of black leather gloves. 'I need you to make the challenge in the traditional way.' She turns back to Jonesy. 'Did you choose your gun?'

'I'm not using a gun.'

'Your choice,' she says. 'But at least this way you have a chance.'

'Screw you,' says Jonesy.

They turn and walk towards the bus station. Mim leans again into her lapel. 'Can you put the snipers on standby, sir? We might have an escape attempt.'

The skinheads stop walking.

'Snipers?' says Jonesy.

'Just a precaution,' says Mim. 'Now, if you choose your gun, we can get started.'

'Look,' says Jonesy, holding out his arms. 'We're sorry, okay.'

'You're sorry? You want to apologise?'

'Yeah, there's no need for any guns.'

'Well, I suppose the challenge hasn't been issued yet. What do you think, Constable?'

'Come on, mate,' Jonesy says, turning to me. 'No one wants a gun fight.'

'He will require a formal apology of course,' says Mim.

'Yeah, of course. Sorry.'

'No,' says Mim. 'I'm afraid it will have to be said using the prescribed words.'

'Eh?'

'We need it for the records. As I said, this is being recorded.'

'Okay. Whatever. Tell me what to say, and I'll say it.'

'Excellent,' says Mim, reaching into the attaché case and pulling out a gold-coloured card. 'It's always better when these things are resolved amicably.' She hands the card to Jonesy. 'You need to read this to Constable Shaw, and then it's up to him whether he forgives you or not.'

'Forgives me?'

Mim puts her finger on the earpiece. 'Yes, sir. We're just negotiating. If you could bear with me for a moment.' She nods to the skinhead. 'Ready when you are.'

Jonesy looks up at the walkway and then down at the card. The rest of the skinheads stand at his side, their arms folded. He starts to read. 'I unreservedly apologise to Constable Shaw–'

'A bit louder please,' says Mim.

'What?'

Mim points upwards. 'For the tape. They're telling me you need to speak up a bit.'

Jonesy coughs. 'I unreservedly apologise to Constable Shaw for my unacceptable and ungentlemanly behaviour. This behaviour will never be repeated, and I humbly request Constable Shaw's forgiveness.'

'Good,' says Mim. 'Well, that sounded pretty sincere to me, Constable. What do you think?'

'I'm not sure he means it,' I say.

'Do you want me to beg, mate?' says Jonesy.

Mim looks at me. 'It's an option I suppose.'

*

My head flops forwards and I wake with a shudder, spittle running from the corner of my mouth. I wipe my lips with the back of my hand and sit up in the seat. My newspaper slides to the floor. I hear the train, de-dum, de-dum, de-dum, de-dum, and feel the rocking motion beneath me. Everything has returned to normal speed. Mim smiles at me from the opposite seat. 'I don't understand,' I say.

She picks up my Guardian, folds it in half and places it in my lap. 'You were dreaming,' she says.

'You were there,' I say. 'Inside my head.'

'Really. What did I do?'

'You said you could help me… and then you took my hand…'

'Did your dream give you a solution?' she says.

'A solution?'

'To your skinhead problem? It sounded a sorry tale.'

I reach into the pocket of my jacket and pull out the handkerchief she gave me. I wipe my mouth again. 'Who are you?' I say.

'You know who I am,' she says. 'I'm a friend who can help you.' She opens the zip on her carpet bag, pulls out a black business card and hands it to me. 'Let me know when you're ready,' she says.

I look at the card. "Guardian Angel" written in gold letters. 'Ready for what?' I say.

'To sort your problem,' she says.

I look again at the card. 'But there's no number. How do I get hold of you?'

'I'll know,' she says, squeezing my hand.

The train slows down.

Mim zips up her bag and stands up. 'This is my stop,' she says.

'You can't just go. I need to know…'

She touches my cheek.

Ten, nine, eight, seven…

I feel the train come to a standstill.

'I'll see you soon,' she whispers in my ear.

I can smell the eucalyptus oil.

Six, five, four…

She throws her bag over her shoulder, straightens her beret, opens the door and leaves the compartment.

I can see Jonesy in my head, Mim in her pinstripe suit, the guns, the apology…

Three, two, one.

Roots

I'm looking through my kitchen window, watching two pigeons rebuild their nest in the oak tree at the bottom of my garden. They pick up bits of wood from the bark chippings, carry them back, land awkwardly in the branches, shuffle through the leaves to find the strongest base, high enough to avoid the cats.

Year after year, a fresh batch of chicks start a new life in this tree, existing as a family until they're able to fly on their own wings.

I turn and face Josh. He's unrolling an A3 sheet of paper across the oak dining table, his face florid with excitement. 'This is amazing,' he says, placing salt and pepper mills in opposite corners to weigh down the family tree. 'Any juicy stories?'

'Yep,' I say, walking over and sitting in the cottage chair next to him. 'Bastards, bigamists, deserters. They're all there.'

'A gift for an author,' he says.

'Absolutely. I'll be using a fair bit of it.'

'Is that ethical? To use your family like that.'

'Ethical? It's fair game if it's out there. Never tell anything to a writer, sweetheart. It'll be taken down and used against you.'

'Good job I've never told you about my secret past.'

'Oh, really,' I say, tickling him. 'You know you can't keep anything from me. You have to tell me everything.'

He grabs my hands, pulls me towards him and kisses me on the lips. 'That's probably true,' he says, looking into my eyes. 'But you never really know, do you?'

'Oh, a mystery man. Go on then. Shock me with your murderous relatives.'

'You tell me yours and I might share,' he says. 'Quid pro quo to quote Dr Lecter.'

My Samsung vibrates across the table.

'Saved by the bell,' he says, looking up at the wall clock. 'That'll be your mum with her eleven o'clock call.'

'This conversation isn't finished,' I say, picking up my phone. 'I'll be torturing you later.'

*

I end the call and put the phone back on the table.

'You okay?' says Josh, squeezing my hand.

'It's Dad. Mum says he's had a stroke, been admitted to a nursing home.'

'I didn't think they were in touch.'

'They're not, but Dad's brother phoned her. Have we got any wine left?'

Josh stands up, walks over to the fridge and fetches out a bottle of Muscadet. He half fills two Jamie Oliver tumblers and hands one to me. I take a gulp, and then another. Josh tops up my glass. 'Will you go and see him?' he says.

'Why would I? I haven't seen him for years. Seems a bit hypocritical to be the caring daughter now.'

'He's still your dad, Nicki.'

'Big deal. He made his choices.' I take another gulp of Muscadet and look at the family tree. 'Turns out Mum's family weren't Black Country dinosaurs. We started life in Norfolk. My two times great granny brought us here on a narrowboat in 1848.'

'Nice story,' says Josh, sitting back down and placing the wine bottle in front of us.

'Yep,' I say. 'We breed strong women. You'd better watch out.'

'I'm not sure you got the water gene,' he says. 'Remember that barge trip last year when you crashed us into the bank? That fisherman's still in therapy.'

'He shouldn't have been fishing there. Anyway, Granny didn't crew the boat. Boatmen did that. That's why I keep you around.'

'To steer your boat?'

'To do stuff, idiot. And pour me wine.'

'Your wish,' he says, topping up my glass.

I pick up the second A3 sheet and unroll it on top of the first.

'That your dad's?' says Josh.

I nod. 'Him and his phoney Northern roots. His family were only in Middlesbrough because, shock of all shocks, Charlie boy, my great grandad, deserted.'

'From the army?'

'From his family. Refused to pay maintenance to his kids. It must run in the genes.'

'You know,' says Josh, taking a sip of wine. 'You've never heard your dad's side of the story.'

'He left me, Josh. There's nothing he can say to make

up for that.'

'I know, but, well, families are complicated. It's rarely straight forward.'

'You think I should pop along to the nursing home, fall into his arms, kiss and make up–'

'You should go and visit him while he's still here to visit.'

'He left me when I was a baby. That's not something you get over.'

'I'm just saying you should think about it. It sounds like you're running out of time.'

*

I stare at my face in the heart-shaped brass mirror and touch my nose. Celestial, Mum calls it. 'You get it from him,' she says. 'It's on the face of his brothers as well. Makes you feel like you're a bad smell when they look at you.' I touch the tip and look sideways in the mirror. Josh likes it, pixie nose he calls it.

'Good morning, Mrs Sadler. I'm Matron.'

I turn. A slim, red-haired woman in a navy-blue nurse uniform, a silver fob watch peeping out from her dress breast pocket. 'Call me Nicki,' I say. 'It always makes me feel like I'm in trouble when I'm given the Mrs title.'

'I understand this is your first visit.'

'Yes,' I say, wondering how much she knows about our history, what Dad's family have said. 'My parents divorced when I was a child.'

'I know,' she says, 'but, to be honest, it's not really any of my business.' She gestures towards two wing-back chairs near the window. We sit down. 'How much do you know about your dad's condition?'

'Not much. His brother told my mum he'd had a stroke, but that's about it really.'

She hesitates. 'It was quite severe I'm afraid, Nicki.'

'You mean he's dying.'

'I mean the stroke has left him vulnerable. We're not sure how much he knows about what's going on, and he's not able to communicate. We have to do everything for him.'

'Oh,' I say. 'I didn't know it was that bad.'

'I thought it best to tell you before you saw him.'

I look around the reception area. Flower-print embossed wallpaper, a six-foot-tall money tree in the far corner, two coded-access doors leading off into the residential units. I feel Matron watching me, waiting for me to say something. 'I'm not sure there's any point then,' I say, standing up.

'I see. You've changed your mind.'

'It was my husband's idea. He said I should talk to Dad before it was too late, but it sounds like that's not possible. I'm sorry to have wasted your time.'

She stands up and takes my hand. 'It's just a short walk down that corridor,' she says, nodding to the right corner of the room. 'You don't have to stay if you don't want to.'

Her hand feels warm.

'I'll stay with you, if that'll help,' she says.

*

The noise of the unit hits me like a tidal wave.

A man in a striped pyjama top sits at a dining table, banging a spoon into an empty dessert dish. 'I want my porridge oats,' he chants. 'I want my porridges oats.' A woman in a light-blue uniform stands by the microwave. 'It's coming, Harry,' she shouts. 'Try and be a little patient.'

In the centre of the lounge, four people – two older women with the same haircut, wearing matching lilac trouser suits, and two women in uniform – sit around a card table playing dominoes. 'No, Sarah,' says one of the uniformed women. 'Don't suck the dominoes. That's dirty.' Sarah cackles, which the other older woman copies to a tee. They burst out laughing and then cackle again and again and again.

Next to them, a man with a Captain Birdseye beard sits cross-legged with his nose pressing against a blank TV screen. 'Come on,' he shouts, hitting his right thigh. 'Come on.' A man in uniform sits on a chair next to him, his hand resting on Captain Birdseye's back. 'The horse racing's not on yet, Arthur,' he says. 'We'll put it on later.'

'Whip him,' shouts Captain Birdseye. 'Whip him hard.'

A scream. One of the uniformed women playing dominoes stands up and races across the lounge. 'Hobby,' she shouts, 'take your hands from Evelyn's throat. That's not very nice, is it?'

Hobby turns and glares through one eye, his left socket completely closed. 'She's pinched it again,' he says. 'Give it back, you cow.'

Evelyn stamps on Hobby's foot. He yells, lets her go. She throws something at him. 'Here's your stinking eye,' she says. 'Next time I'll put it in your tea.'

I feel Matron touch my arm. 'It's always a bit raucous this time of day,' she says. 'It'll calm down in a minute.'

'What's wrong with them?'

'Dementia, mostly.'

'And this is where Dad's living?'

'It's the unit with most staff,' she says. 'And your dad needs a lot of care.'

I look around the lounge again. 'Why are those old women dressed the same?'

'Oh,' says Matron, 'they're sisters. The only way to stop them fighting is to make sure they have everything in duplicate, even their food.'

'Jesus,' I say.

'Your dad's over there,' says Matron, smiling.

I follow her across the lounge.

She stops at the side of an old man sat in a bucket seat by the window, a restraining belt fixed around his waist. He looks wedged in the chair, like someone has dropped him from a great height. Gloopy streams of saliva drip over his lips, across his chin, and drop onto the blue plastic bib around his neck. Matron pulls out a paper tissue from the box of Kleenex on the coffee table and wipes his mouth. 'Terry,' she says, taking his hand. 'This is your daughter, Nicki.'

I kneel down and take Dad's other hand. 'Hello, Dad,' I say.

He returns my squeeze, which makes a lump leap into my throat.

*

The noise eases.

Harry's porridge ping settles him; Hobby and Evelyn sit side by side in lounge chairs, holding hands, looking like newbie couples, one of the staff having wiped Hobby's eye on a tea towel and popped it back where it lives; the sisters have finished their dominoes and now stand at the sink, both drying dishes, the member of staff making sure she hands them the same item of crockery at the same time. The only noise comes from the TV, the horse racing commentary filling the lounge, Arthur sitting in front of the screen, silently pulling at his beard.

I try to imagine what it might be like living here, the staff thinking what they see is what you are, what your life has been, never knowing anything other than the last few months and weeks as your days draw to a close, families telling their version of you.

Dad moves his right foot slightly. I look at him. Nothing. Silence. His world confined to the thoughts inside his head. I wonder what he thinks of me, if he still remembers the five-year-old girl who he tried to see for the first couple of months after he left. Saturday visits to McDonalds for Happy Meals, Mum questioning me about his latest when I got back home, all coming to an end when I cried uncontrollably, and he stopped picking me up.

And then he moved away, found a new life.

'I'll leave you to it for a while,' says Matron, putting a dining chair next to Dad's bucket seat. 'The staff are here if you need them.'

'I'm not sure what to say to him.'

'You don't need to say anything. Just carry on holding his hand.'

She walks away across the lounge.

I sit down. 'Looks like I've left it too late, Dad.'

His glassy eyes stare vacantly around the room. Mum's tears bubble to the surface, the wasted years she spent waiting for him, the kids at school chanting "no dad" at me, Mum's brother giving me away on my wedding day.

'He knows you're here,' says a voice from behind me.

The member of staff who'd been helping the sisters at the kitchen sink walks over to me, the sisters now sitting at a dining table holding hands and humming to each other. 'Barbara,' she says. 'I'm guessing you're Terry's daughter.'

'Yes,' I say. 'Not really sure what I'm doing here.'

'You're visiting your dad. That's the most natural thing in the world, isn't it?'

'It's complicated,' I say.

She pulls a dining chair over and sits beside me. 'You arrived at a bad time. It's not always that crazy.'

'I thought they'd all be knitting.'

Barbara laughs. 'I wouldn't want to give Evelyn any ideas about piercing Hobby's eye.'

'They seem happy enough now,' I say, nodding over to Hobby and Evelyn, who are still holding hands.

'Oh, they love each other to bits. They've been married for over fifty years.'

I look at Dad. 'I've not seen him since I was a kid.'

'Is your mum still alive?'

'And well. She remarried.'

'Your dad doesn't get many visitors. His brother comes, but no one else.'

'Story of his life,' I say. 'Frightened of commitment. In the end, that gets you to loneliness.'

I feel her looking at me.

'Sorry,' I say. 'I'm a writer. Saying things like that becomes a habit.'

'A writer?' says Barbara.

'Yep. For my sins.'

'You know your dad's written a book,' she says.

*

Boris, my tomcat, meows at the back door, with occasional threatening glances towards his litter tray. 'No you don't,' says Josh, jumping out of his chair. 'That tray's for emergencies only.'

Boris looks at him as he opens the door, snarls a meow and stumbles over the step.

'That cat hates me,' he says.

'I don't blame him,' I say. 'It's raining out there.'

'He's a cat,' says Josh.

'It's still raining. How would you like to pee outside in the rain?'

'I'd probably prefer it to peeing in that litter tray.'

He closes the door and sits back down next to me.

'So,' he says, 'your dad's magnum opus. Looks like it's done the rounds.'

I touch the manuscript on the table in front of us. Dog-eared pages, yellow-brown foxing, a coffee cup stain in the middle of the front sheet. 'I wonder when he wrote it,' I say. 'It looks like he's left it in the sun, probably on a shelf somewhere.'

'Did they know anything more at the care home?' says Josh.

I shake my head. 'Nothing. They found it in his

suitcase.' I run my finger over the title and read out loud. 'A Life of Fractures.'

'Looks like you get to find out about him in his own words,' says Josh.

I turn over the front page and read the dedication. 'For my daughter, Nicki. I wish I could have been a better dad.'

Josh puts his arm around me and kisses the top of my head. 'It's a lovely thing to find,' he says. 'Will you read it straight away?'

'I'm not sure. It seems strange to read it while he's still here.'

'I don't understand,' says Josh.

'I've spent all those years hating him, and this might change everything.'

'That's good, isn't it?'

'Not the state he's in, Josh. I can't talk to him now.'

'He wrote it for you, sweetheart. You should read it and tell him you've read it. We'll deal with all the emotions that come out of it.'

I look again at the dedication. 'You know,' I say, 'he could have just told me this stuff. But, no, he has to write a bloody great book. Is there something wrong with men? Why can't you just say what you're feeling?'

Josh shrugs. 'Between you and the cat, I do well to get a word in edgeways in this house.'

I turn over the page. "Chapter One – Childhood".

'You'd better open a bottle of wine,' I say.

Invisible Game

4pm.

Rocky leans back in his office chair, screws the final demand letter into a ball, takes aim and chucks it dead centre into a metal wastepaper basket. The basket rocks once, twice, threatens to topple over, but then rights itself. 'There,' says Rocky. 'Filed and dealt with.'

'Is that a good idea?' says Tina, rolling a piece of Wrigley's around her mouth and running her hand through her Annie-Lennox-style spiky blonde hair. 'They'll cut you off.'

'No choice, darling. We're broke.'

'Something'll turn up. Usually does.'

Rocky shakes his head. 'Not this time. Ghost hunting is dead. No one cares. They're too busy surviving this life to think about the next.'

'You should've stuck to window cleaning,' says Tina. 'You had a nice round going there.'

'Thanks for that, but it's not you who has to drag up and down that ladder in all weathers.'

'I do my bit.'

He opens the bottom drawer of the desk, fetches out a bottle of Johnnie Walker, unscrews the lid and half fills the tumbler in front of him. He takes a drink, looks up at the ceiling and lets the whisky warm the back of his throat. He swallows and takes another drink.

'That's not going to help,' says Tina, walking over to the desk.

'It's making me feel a hell of a lot better,' says Rocky.

She stands behind his chair and starts stroking his hair. 'This isn't like you, babe.'

'We're finished,' he says. 'We haven't had an order for months. Even the cat brigade have stopped asking me to check if Tiddles wants to say a last goodbye. I'm telling you, we need that phone to ring now and give us some work or we're out on our ear.'

His Samsung mobile lights up.

Springsteen's "Born in the USA" bursts into the room.

*

1am.

Rocky looks around the lounge – cobwebs hang from the coving; shimmers of dust cover every surface; the only light comes from a purple-shaded standard lamp by the fireplace, a low-watt bulb forcing elongated shadows of Murano glass ornaments to stretch a path across the carpet. He presses Tina's name on his Samsung. She answers after two rings. 'How's it going?' she says.

'This house is really spooky, babe,' says Rocky. 'No wonder the old man's jumpy.'

'But he's given you the money?'

'Three days up front. I think he's loaded.'

'Then don't mess it up. And stay off the booze.'

'Trust me,' he says. 'This one's a dead cert.' He presses the phone closer to his ear. 'Say the magic words, darling,' he whispers.

'I'm keeping it warm for you,' says Tina.

'That's my girl,' he says. 'I'll be there first thing.'

He pats the top of the monitor on the glass-topped coffee table in front of him, slides the phone into the front pocket of his jeans, picks up the remains of a double Monterey Jack burger from its polystyrene container and tosses the food into his mouth.

The grandfather clock tick, tick, ticks away in the corner of the room.

Ghosts.

He always knew there'd be weirdos ready to part with their hard earned cash for a chat with a corpse. Feed their hope, and the suckers will pay. This could go on for weeks if he deals the right hand. Dare he risk getting Mr Walker out of the van? No. Tina's right. He needs to stay professional.

A shiver races through his body. Goosebumps smother his bare arms. He pulls down his Black Sabbath T-shirt over his hairy paunch, wipes grease from his chin with the back of his hand and squeezes his buttocks into the seat of a tweed-covered wing-back chair. He closes his eyes and feels the draw of his favourite dream, Debbie Harry pulling his head towards her. 'Kiss me,' she says.

'Is everything okay, young man?'

'Jesus, Ned,' says Rocky, opening his eyes. 'You scared the crap out of me.'

'Sorry,' says Ned, tightening the belt on his dressing

gown. 'I couldn't sleep.' He nods at the monitor. 'You getting anything?'

'Not yet,' says Rocky, sitting up and reaching for his pack of ever-faithful More menthol. 'They're unpredictable things, spooks. Invisible prey, unless you know what you're doing.'

'You've hunted a lot then?'

'Yeah. Stop worrying. If they're here, I'll get them. There's motion detectors in every room. Nothing squeaks in this house without it being trapped by me. You go back to bed and leave it to the experts.'

'I'll keep you company,' says Ned, sitting down on the settee. 'Unless that interferes with things.'

'Please yourself,' says Rocky, tossing a cigarette into his mouth. He picks up a box of Swan Vesta, strikes a match, lights the tobacco, squints as he takes a drag, the smoke drifting back into his face. 'You've never actually seen anything,' he says. 'Just heard noises.'

'That's right,' says Ned. 'I feel a bit of a fool now. I'm probably wasting your time.'

'You did the right thing calling me,' says Rocky, patting Ned's leg. 'Can't put a price on peace of mind.'

'It's not as though anything's happened really,' says Ned. 'Apart from the blood.'

'Blood. You never mentioned anything about blood.'

'Didn't I? I meant to. It's happened a couple of times. I've heard a noise in the bathroom, middle of the night, got up to investigate and, there it is, in the loo, streaks of the stuff.'

'That's different,' says Rocky, taking another drag. 'You're sure it's not from you?'

'No, son. I'm alright in that department.'

'And that's it? Just the noises and blood.'

'Nothing else,' says Ned. 'Any idea what it means?'

Rocky leans back in the chair. Blood. Crazy old man. Forget weeks. This job could go on for months. 'It could be more complicated than we thought,' he says. 'I might need some more equipment.'

*

3am.

Jasmine, lemon and vanilla perfume lace the air.

Rocky's phut, phut, phut snoring beats out its gentle rhythm.

The monitor crackles into life.

'Wake up,' says Ned, shaking Rocky. 'She's here. She's in the bathroom.'

'What?' says Rocky, rubbing his eyes and looking at the screen.

A flickering head and shoulders shadow anchors itself on the white porcelain tiles. A woman, long blonde hair, pinstripe suit, white shirt, black tie, reaches over the bath and turns on the shower. It gushes into life. A hand looms out of the monitor and knocks three times on the glass.

Rocky grabs Ned's arm. 'Who's in the house?' he says. 'Who else is here?'

'No one,' says Ned.

The tapping sounds again. The grandfather clock stops ticking. Someone turns off the shower. The woman's face, chalky white, translucent skin, black eye sockets, rictus grin, fills the screen. The lights in the bathroom go out. The shower restarts.

'If this is your idea of a joke, old man,' says Rocky, jumping out of his seat.

'It's the ghost,' says Ned. 'She's in the bathroom. Aren't you going to get up there?'

Rocky looks at the screen again. He can hear the shower through the monitor's speakers. The bathroom is still in darkness. A scream echoes around the house.

'What the fuck?' says Rocky, looking at Ned. 'You're sure this isn't a wind-up?'

'I swear,' says Ned. 'There's no one here but us.'

'And this is what's happened before?'

'Not like this. The shower, yes, but never the scream.'

Rocky picks up a brass candlestick off the sideboard and looks at Ned. 'Maybe we should call the police.'

'And say what. There's never anything there apart from the blood. We should at least have a look.'

'Okay,' says Rocky, 'but you wait here.'

'No way,' says Ned. 'I'm coming with you. I want to find out what's going on. Anyway, you might need some help.'

The scream rings out again.

Rocky walks towards the lounge door, still gripping the candlestick. He stops, turns back and faces Ned. 'You stay right back, old man. I don't want anything happening to you while I'm here.'

'I will,' says Ned. 'I will.'

The shower stops.

*

They creep up the stairs, ascending the darkness, the only light coming from the hallway below, the silhouette of a landing balustrade dropping onto the opposite wall, pictures of long-dead relatives hanging precariously along the flock wallpaper route, staring out with penetrating eyes and knowing grins.

Ned grips the stair rail for support, keeping two steps behind Rocky, who is holding the candlestick above his head.

'You sure we can't get any light up here?' says Rocky, grinding to a halt.

'The switch is on the landing,' says Ned. 'Don't you have a torch?'

'It's in the van. Didn't think I'd need it,' says Rocky, looking at the brass stick. 'It's a pity we didn't get a candle for this thing.'

'I might have some in the kitchen. Shall I look?'

Rocky shakes his head and then remembers his phone. He reaches into his pocket, pulls out the Samsung, scrolls down the screen and presses the torch icon. He hands the phone to Ned. 'You keep this light shining in front of us.'

Ned nods and holds the torch towards the landing. The beam of light picks out a yucca plant in a green flowerpot, perched on a stool in front of them. 'Why's it so bloody cold?' says Rocky.

'It shouldn't be,' says Ned. 'The central heating's on. I normally turn it off at night, but with you being here…'

'Right,' says Rocky, hoicking up his jeans and turning back towards the landing.

'What's wrong?' says Ned.

'I just need a second. This doesn't feel right.'

'I thought you'd done this loads of times.'

'I have, but that scream, and the blood. You sure there's no one else in the house?'

'No one. Just you and me.'

'Okay, but you stay back until we find out what's going on.'

'Anything you say,' says Ned.

They carry on, one hesitant step at a time.

Rocky reaches the landing.

'The light switch is on the wall in front of you,' says Ned.

Rocky finds the switch, presses it down. Nothing. He presses it again. Off, on, off, on… still nothing. 'It's not working,' he says.

'Let me try,' says Ned, walking onto the landing and pressing the switch. Off, on, off, on… nothing. He looks at Rocky. 'It was fine earlier,' he says.

A scream echoes around the house.

'What the fuck is that?' says Rocky.

'It's coming from the bathroom,' says Ned, nodding at the closed door in front of them.

Rocky steps forward, puts his hand on the doorknob.

The shower restarts.

He lets go of the knob and steps back. 'This is some weird shit you've got here,' he says. 'We should call the police.'

'You can't stop now,' says Ned. 'At least open the door.'

Rocky looks at the doorknob, the candlestick held out in front of him. It can't be real. There must be some obvious explanation. The old man's right. The police would laugh. And he'd never be able to do this job again. A ghost hunter afraid of ghosts. He'd look a right dick. 'I thought I told you to stand back,' he says, facing Ned.

Ned nods and steps back towards the stairs.

'Keep that torch shining in front of me,' says Rocky, turning back to the door.

He takes a deep breath, puts his hand back on the doorknob, turns and pushes.

The bathroom lights come on.

The woman in a pinstripe suit screams, stands up off the toilet, races towards the landing, click-clacking a pair of garden shears in front of her, heading for Rocky's eyes.

*

The smell of jasmine, lemon and vanilla cloys him, making him want to retch. His head is pumped with fear, danger, danger, danger. He feels something waft a draught across his face. He's not fully sure where he is, but he knows he must run, get away from here, get away from here now. At work. The old man. And… oh my God. His eyes shoot open.

Ned stands over him, flapping a towel. 'Are you okay, son? You frightened the life out of me.'

Rocky sits up and looks around. He's lying on the landing, outside the bathroom. 'That woman,' he says. 'She ran straight at me.'

'Easy,' says Ned, putting his hand on Rocky's back. 'Take some deep breaths.'

Rocky's startled eyes scan the landing. He turns his body sharply to look down the stairs, the bathroom light joining up with the hall lamp to illuminate the scene. 'Where's she gone? What's happened to her?'

'Who?' says Ned, dropping the tea towel to his side.

'She was right there, in the bathroom. You must have seen her. She had a pair of shears for God's sake.'

'All I saw was you opening the door and then dropping to the floor. I thought you'd fainted.'

Rocky rubs his head and struggles to his feet. He walks into the bathroom and looks around. Shower off, window wide open. An ambulance screams past the house, its siren blaring out. 'She was right there,' he says, pointing at the toilet. 'And the screaming, you heard the screaming.'

'We got ourselves worked up,' says Ned, walking to his side. 'The scream could have been next door's tomcats fighting.'

'Cats? What about the face, the shower? You were the one who woke me up, telling me to get up here.'

'The shower's been dodgy for weeks and, to be honest, I never really saw the face.'

'We both saw it. Downstairs. On the monitor.'

'You saw it and, well, you seemed so sure. I thought you must be right.'

'No way,' says Rocky. 'What about the blood? You told me about the blood.'

'I might have exaggerated that a bit,' says Ned, looking at the floor. 'I wanted to spice things up a bit, get you to take me seriously. I didn't think you'd react like you did.'

Rocky grabs Ned's dressing gown and pulls him into his face. 'You mean this has all been a game,' splutters Rocky, spittle landing on Ned's nose. 'I nearly had a stroke you crazy old bastard.'

'I'm sorry,' says Ned.

'Screw that,' says Rocky, pushing Ned against the wall and storming off down the stairs.

*

The grandfather clock tick, tick, ticks away in the corner of the lounge.

Rocky disconnects the monitor and starts winding up the cables, adrenalin speeding through his body, feeding his escape – do something, do anything to get away – his heart banging out of his chest. He splutters, grabs his mouth to smother a cry, sits down in the wing-back chair and puts his head in his hands. The face, the rictus grin, the shears clack, clack, clacking towards him.

'I'm sorry if I frightened you,' says Ned, leaning against the door frame. 'Can I come in?'

'It's your house,' says Rocky, wiping his eyes. 'You can do what you want.'

Ned walks over to a walnut writing bureau, opens the roller door and pulls out a flat surface of wood. He sets up a bottle of Glenmorangie and two tumblers. 'Drink?' he says, holding out the bottle. 'It's meant to be good for shock.'

Rocky nods.

Ned splashes whisky into both of the tumblers, hands one to Rocky and then sits down on the settee. They take a drink. 'It seems silly you giving up now,' says Ned. 'I still think there's a ghost.'

'I know there's a ghost,' says Rocky, taking another drink. 'It's you that seems unsure all of a sudden.'

'I just didn't see what you saw,' says Ned. 'You might be more sensitive to that kind of stuff. It is your job.'

'None of what you said makes sense,' says Rocky. 'Those screams, there's no way that was cats. And what about the lights? Or have they been a bit dodgy as well?'

'I can't explain that,' says Ned.

'And that face,' says Rocky. 'You saw that on the monitor. Why are you lying?'

'I'm not,' says Ned. 'I'm saying there *is* a ghost. I just didn't see one tonight. Like I said, it's your job…'

'There's something wrong here, old man.'

'Then stay for a few nights and help me sort it,' says Ned. 'Wouldn't it help your business if you could crack this case?'

*

4am.

Ned looks at the framed photo he's holding in his hand and traces his finger around the woman's face. 'Beautiful,' he says.

'Where did you find him?' says Alice, looking up from her knitting.

'He's got a "Ghouls R Us" logo in the Yellow Pages.'

'How exciting,' she says, rocking her chair.

'Not really. He's a charlatan, but the game relieved the boredom for a couple of hours. He's coming back tonight. We'll have to see what else we can conjure up for him.'

She stands up and walks over to the window. Ned puts his arm around her shoulder, and she snuggles into his chest. He looks over at the dressing table. A bell-shaped bottle of Shalimar perfume sits centre stage in the mirror. He takes a deep breath.

Two sprays every morning is all it takes to bring Alice back.

They watch in silence as Rocky drags his trolley-load of equipment down the driveway back to his white transit van. The wheels of the trolley wedge in the flint chippings; Rocky stumbles. Alice laughs.

Ned squeezes her closer and kisses the top of her head.

'I miss you,' he says. 'I will always miss you.'

It all seemed idyllic, until it wasn't.

Seven years of age, Dad died, and I left the world, retreated inwards, became terrified of the dark – leave the light on, Mum. Leave the light on. It felt like I'd been sucked into a black hole, falling, falling, falling. My life stolen. I stopped going out, drifted around in Enid Blyton's Famous Five, talked non-stop to my teddies, missed months and months of school with a mystery back pain, lying on the settee, making safe worlds with my cowboys and Indians, occasionally venturing outside to chat with the clouds, which is where I thought Dad had gone.

Jack tried, but I wasn't there.

He called, knocked the landing window, his grubby face gurning at me, but I hid under the blankets, and he moved on, found another kid, Rob Cooper, to share his life.

I became a loner, a mummy's boy.

By the time I resurfaced, we were moving up the pseudo-social ladder.

My last memory of Jack is him and Rob Cooper visiting me in the new flat. They'd walked six miles to satisfy their curiosity. They knocked over all the potted plants in the communal area and called me a posh twat.

I write it all down.

My stomach is griping. I feel my tumour moving around, stretching out, poking its poison into my internal organs. It makes sense. It's alive. Curiosity must make it want to explore its new world. Perhaps I should let it. After all, I'm its host, and hosts need to entertain their guests.

My right hand starts to tremor.

Cancer grabs my gut.

Coats for Goalposts

A wing-back chair, a woollen bed blanket in case I feel a chill, a three-times-per-day wait for the home care, a vase of daffodils on the sideboard, a bottle of morphine on the coffee table.

My second-floor view is a bus stop, people waiting in all weathers, clutching their plastic carrier bags, sharing gossip, returning hours later, unloading themselves onto the opposite pavement, repeating it all tomorrow and tomorrow and tomorrow.

Cancer moves through my body, munching me. My hand reaches out for more morphine, wanting to thwart the stabbing, deny it the pleasure of snatching my breath. I tell myself to wait. There's an hour to go before I'm due a dose, and too much knocks me for six, wastes a day from my reducing quota.

A distraction, try to think of something else.

Death makes me think about life. Maybe this is where we all wash up, watching the world, reflecting, waiting for the end. I've got my memories. Good and bad. I found a way to survive. I've loved and been loved. There's a lot that can't say that. On the whole, I've done okay, but I want to make some sense of what's happened to me, make a record of my crossroad choices, left or right, ponder about different paths I might have taken.

Cancer makes people stay away. Cancer. People mouth the word rather than say it out loud. Any word association game would follow it with death. It conjures up a shroud of fear, best to be avoided. Stay away. Stay away. Not that I had many people to scare. I've lived a life without acquiring friends, but I don't think I'm on my own. Most people seem friendless these days, unless you count the feigned recesses of social media where the only contact is an emoji.

I open my half-filled purple moleskin notebook, pick up my Parker cartridge pen, write "True Friends" at the top of the page and then stare out of the window, trying to work out when I had someone that close, sharing my world, watching my back, me watching theirs, gravity pulling us in exactly the same orbit.

Jack.

We rolled in common childhood dirt, our births separated by two months and twenty feet of driveway, both of us born at home. He had fourteen siblings. I had two, but with a ten- and fifteen-year gap between me and my brother and sister, I might as well have been an only child. Our families shared a history of friendship. His brothers and sisters hung around with my brother and sister, and we were expected to follow the pattern.

He became my surrogate sibling.

Our lives were spent in each other's shadow, mouthing off at Mr Perry when he threatened to put a knitting needle through our Casey ball; the day someone slide tackled me on the concrete and I fractured my elbow; our plant raids around the neighbours' gardens, trying to get some colour

back home; the day I jumped off a swing and fractured my wrist.

Jack used to climb on the porch roof and knock our landing window, directly opposite my bedroom. I'd get up, get dressed and out we'd go. Bike rides to Livingston Green, the journey there and back taking us forever; the day his brother, Charlie, took us to Cannock Chase, my mum worried sick because she thought Charlie wasn't the full shilling. I touch the scar on my forehead and smile – a trophy from the day Jack pushed me into his front door because I wouldn't share my biscuits.

I can't remember it raining when we shared the world. Sun, wind, ice, snow, but never rain. Everything happened outside. Kite flying, crossbows, bow and arrows, all home-made in my mum's back kitchen from pieces of wood string, newspaper and old bits of elastic; British Bulldo the last kid to try and make it across the green crushed b fifteen other kids tripping, punching, swearing, trying inflict the greatest physical damage – if you were sm you got caught early. Hours and hours of just being ki Marbles, conkers, swopping stickers – got, got, got – a of course, every day we could, football.

Leeds United. I'd never been outside of Walsall, they were my obsession. I still recall the team that wo 1972 FA Cup final, which Jack and I watched on a b and-white TV in my mum's sitting room, trying to so aerial, to stop the picture rolling and four shadows of Jones running up the pitch. When we played on the I became Alan "Sniffer" Clarke, a goal poacher, or Lorimer, a toe punter. I remember Jack crossing th Georgie Best style, and me scoring from a bicycle k

I pick up the medicine pot, ready filled with ten mils of clear elixir, and gulp down the morphine. My face instinctively winces, always expecting bitterness, but it tastes of nothing, just slides down my throat, warming as it goes on its seek-and-find mission.

The hit registers in my brain.

I look out of the window.

At least the drizzle's stopped. Gives me a better chance of seeing some exotic birds through this pair of binoculars Claire, the home carer, gave me. 'It'll relieve the boredom,' she said. 'But no spying on the neighbours. I don't want any complaints about a Peeping Tom.' I bought a book, The A-Z of British Birds, but Passer domesticus, or the common house sparrow, is about as exotic as it gets. Still, what did I expect through a Walsall lounge window?

Birdwatching.

A council estate kid now a twitcher, checking out Latin names.

My buddy after Jack would have been impressed.

I put my hand on my stomach.

The morphine seems to have found its target.

I pick up my notebook.

Freddie.

Strange fish from very different ponds, but our worlds collided for a while in the 1970s. I blame Mum. She landed on her feet with the housing list after Dad died. 'You're lucky to get this,' said Roger from the neighbourhood office. 'They don't come up very often.'

Lucky. A shitty token gesture of three, three-storey blocks of council flats in a middle-class affluent suburb. Two bedrooms, rotting window frames, wallpaper sliding off the running-water-covered plaster, black mould sticking to my clothes, underfloor heating no one could use without robbing a bank to pay the bill. I lay in bed during the winter months, listening to Mum crying in the bathroom, her hands in hot water, trying to settle her ravaged arthritis. She tried to get a councillor on her side. Roger gave her a diary, a bottle of spray for the mould, told her to put on an extra jumper, to fill the holes in the frames with toilet tissue. She pushed her luck, went back. He gave her a dehumidifier, a fortune to run and useless against the tide of damp. 'You've moved up in the world, Mrs,' said Roger. 'Try and enjoy it.'

That's how Freddie and I came into the same orbit.

We went to Manor Farm Comp but never mixed there. His form had posh, nerdy kids who wore glasses, washed, had their clothes ironed, ticked the career officer's "this one has prospects" box; my form had the rest, the ones with nicknames like Tramp, the cocks of the school, the ones whose dads served at Her Majesty's pleasure. I clung like shitty pants to the third best fighter in our year, making me untouchable, out of everyone's reach, something that came back to bite me when I tried to return for sixth form, me exposed, but that's a different story.

My friendship with Freddie existed extra-curricular. He lived on a different planet, six bedrooms, opposite the golf course, municipal park-sized back garden, pull-on pull-off drive, radiators in every room, shower in the bathroom. His dad a company director who drove a Volvo estate, his mum a PA, holidays abroad every year, Malta, new trainers, leather bomber jacket, 501 jeans, season ticket holder at The Baggies.

I became his bit of rough.

At the end of each day, we got off the school bus at the last stop and headed for the newsagent. Cadbury's creme eggs for me, Express and Star paper for him. That's how we got talking, chatting on the wall by the OAP flats. Music, Yvonne Elliman for him, Elkie Brooks for me; TV, Dallas – who shot JR? Bobby's shower resurrection – Minder, That's Life, Rising Damp – he did a wonderful Leonard Rossiter impression, hands on hips, goofy grin, oh, Miss Jones.

Freddie's looks were more Kays Catalogue than street. His curtain hairstyle, long before David Beckham, held in place by copious resprays of Silvikrin. Roughing up his hair pissed him off, but he just pulled a comb out of his back pocket, found a mirror and reset it. Suddenly, girls who were way out of my league would shout at me in a plummy accent, "where's your mate?", "tell Freddie I said hello". He'd shrug when I told him and then tell me some football story.

He walked down most evenings from his oasis on the hill and sat in our flat, drinking tea and eating fondant fancies from Marks and Spencer, all served by my mum. He stayed over one night after we'd watched a Friday night Frankenstein film. We shared my single bed, sleeping top and tail. It never happened again. He said my feet stank.

We bunked off school, jumped on a bus to anywhere, nowhere, paid the minimum fare, camped out on the upstairs back seat, ignored the smell-cocktail of nicotine, piss and body odour soaking into the fabric, saw how far we could get before they kicked us off. Tamworth made us late home. The bus journeys stopped, but not the bunking off. We hid away in my mum's flat, him putting his feet up on our battered leather settee. The inevitable happened. His mum had a phone call from the school, turned up at the flat and drove us both to the headmaster. Two things I remember from that day: the school hadn't phoned my mum – I wasn't the one with prospects – and how incredibly sweet and polite Freddie's mum was, not shouting, staying calm, never telling my mum what had happened.

Kindness ran in his family. He helped my brother move house. We lay in the back of the empty removal van as my brother drove it, at speed, back to the hire company, our feet up on the sides, feeling every bump in the road, rolling with every turn, singing Racey's "Lay Your Love on Me" and Darts' "Come Back My Love".

Football dominated our time. Just the two of us, one-to-one combat in the nets, a sunken concrete park on the edge of the estate that you reached by walking down steps off the pavement. Freddie would stand one end of an area the size of a tennis court, me at the other, coats and jumpers setting out our individual goal behind us. You could score from a distance, but getting close up, tackling, chipping, swerving made it more likely. Losing the ball on the attack meant you were vulnerable, your own goal wide open. It went on for hours, only darkness bringing it to a close. In all the time we played, I don't remember seeing another person using the park. We had our own private playground, playing a game we'd designed ourselves.

A perfect existence, which soured in the adult world.

The end built up slowly, over weeks. The dole picked me up, queuing outside the labour exchange, clutching my

UB40, chatting to my mates from school, the ones who weren't in borstal. Freddie worked for his dad, meaning he could spend his days getting paid to restudy for his O levels, which we'd both failed. He joined the golf club, passed his driving test first time; his dad bought him a new yellow Datsun. I failed my driving test three times, passed on the fourth and, with the help of my mum, bought a rusted-up Morris Marina, which spent most of its mechanical failure life parked up kerbside outside our block of flats because I couldn't afford the petrol.

We still played football in the nets, but it became all I had. My head filled with his privilege, his leather jacket, training shoes, big house, golf, holidays abroad, new car, his moneybags dad. It knitted together, fuelling my rage. I kicked the ball harder, ran faster, fought for possession, tripped him up, demanded another game, and another and another. 'Calm down,' he said.

'It's you,' I said. 'You're getting soft in that office.'

He told me to piss off.

I ran over and punched him in the face.

I can still see the look he gave me as he held his nose, blood trickling through his fingers, like something in the world had fractured. I held up my hands and said sorry, but he shook his head and ran out of the park. Two days later, I walked up to his house. His mum answered the door, asked how I was, told me Freddie didn't want to see me, and then she said, 'Friendships do come to an end, you know.'

I didn't call again, and neither did he.

Friendships.

I write it all down.

Jack and Freddie.

We're sixty this year. I wonder where they are, what paths they travelled, what cards life dealt them. I hope they're okay. Stephen Hawking always talked about parallel universes where every moment in time continues to exist, being played over and over on a loop. I like to think that's true, that somewhere Freddie and I are still kicking a ball at each other in the nets, that Jack and I are still flying our kites. I suppose, looking back, the comfort is we found each other at all, that for a nanosecond of time our paths crossed.

I close the notebook.

Sleep drops my head forward, but I wake myself with a start. The notebook thuds as it hits the floor. I feel a flush rising up my body; sweat beads pop on my forehead. I reach towards the coffee table. Not yet. It's barely been twenty minutes since my last fix. A pinch in my stomach, a gentle prod. A reminder of my guest.

I look at the notebook.

No more writing. I can't do any more today.

The bus is back.

My neighbour, Ted, lands on the pavement, his hand in the air waving at me from the street. A distraction. He'll do. He talks. I listen. Tells me all about his holidays in the Maldives, shows me snap, after snap, after snap.

I force myself out of the chair and walk towards the front door.

I'll catch him on the landing if I'm lucky.

Locked In

A constant throbbing in my head, stiffness in my fingers, machines beeping, the white noise of a clunk, clunk, clunking respirator, waking up but not being awake. I'm punctured like a colander – stomach, throat, veins. Everything going in and out needs help. A tracheotomy blowhole in the front of my neck squirts phlegm.

Two nurses chatter over me. 'Do you think she can hear us?'

'They say she can, but she can't.'

'Her daughter sits for hours talking to her.'

'Fair play. Don't think I'd have the patience.'

'I heard the dad was some kind of war hero. Got himself killed.'

'Poor cow.'

They touch me, roll my carcass, scrunch a sheet against my back. Yank. Another roll. Yank. Another. It's over, except it isn't. They seize me by the shoulders, pull me forward, untie the gown at the back of my neck, slide it down my deadweight arms, drop me flat. I bounce slightly as my naked, paralysed body hits the mattress. A soapy flannel squelches against me.

No words.

A hard towel scrubs me dry; cold creams slap under my breasts; plastic gloves slip across my skin. They grab my shoulders, pull me up again; a new gown covers my bare flesh. A comb scrapes through my hair.

'That's her done.'

'Bloody good job. She gives me the creeps.'

'I know what you mean. It's like laying out a slab of sirloin every morning.'

The door slams.

I hear trolleys clattering in the corridor; the smell of antiseptic cloys. I try to move a part of me, anything. Nothing. Not even my eyelids. I crave for a stretch. The only view I have is inside my head, the only movement, a nanosecond blink in my big toe, which I repeat over and over. It's a start.

The door opens.

'Hello, Mum.'

Molly.

She squeezes my hand.

*

Molly sits at my bedside most days, talking about her childhood, me brush, brush, brushing her hair; the sailor's outfit I made her wear for a portrait picture when she was two, chubby legs squeezed by tight white socks, burgundy buckle shoes pinching her feet – 'You gave everybody a copy, Mum. It's so embarrassing,' – my bread-and-butter pudding, which she says I never told her how to make; the Christmas tree decorations we bought on holiday in the Isle of Wight; her fifth birthday when I lost her in St Ives

Coats for Goalposts

A wing-back chair, a woollen bed blanket in case I feel a chill, a three-times-per-day wait for the home care, a vase of daffodils on the sideboard, a bottle of morphine on the coffee table.

My second-floor view is a bus stop, people waiting in all weathers, clutching their plastic carrier bags, sharing gossip, returning hours later, unloading themselves onto the opposite pavement, repeating it all tomorrow and tomorrow and tomorrow.

Cancer moves through my body, munching me. My hand reaches out for more morphine, wanting to thwart the stabbing, deny it the pleasure of snatching my breath. I tell myself to wait. There's an hour to go before I'm due a dose, and too much knocks me for six, wastes a day from my reducing quota.

A distraction, try to think of something else.

Death makes me think about life. Maybe this is where we all wash up, watching the world, reflecting, waiting for the end. I've got my memories. Good and bad. I found a way to survive. I've loved and been loved. There's a lot that can't say that. On the whole, I've done okay, but I want to make some sense of what's happened to me, make a record of my crossroad choices, left or right, ponder about different paths I might have taken.

Cancer makes people stay away. Cancer. People mouth the word rather than say it out loud. Any word association game would follow it with death. It conjures up a shroud of fear, best to be avoided. Stay away. Stay away. Not that I had many people to scare. I've lived a life without acquiring friends, but I don't think I'm on my own. Most people seem friendless these days, unless you count the feigned recesses of social media where the only contact is an emoji.

I open my half-filled purple moleskin notebook, pick up my Parker cartridge pen, write "True Friends" at the top of the page and then stare out of the window, trying to work out when I had someone that close, sharing my world, watching my back, me watching theirs, gravity pulling us in exactly the same orbit.

Jack.

We rolled in common childhood dirt, our births separated by two months and twenty feet of driveway, both of us born at home. He had fourteen siblings. I had two, but with a ten- and fifteen-year gap between me and my brother and sister, I might as well have been an only child. Our families shared a history of friendship. His brothers and sisters hung around with my brother and sister, and we were expected to follow the pattern.

He became my surrogate sibling.

Our lives were spent in each other's shadow, mouthing off at Mr Perry when he threatened to put a knitting needle through our Casey ball; the day someone slide tackled me on the concrete and I fractured my elbow; our plant raids around the neighbours' gardens, trying to get some colour

back home; the day I jumped off a swing and fractured my wrist.

Jack used to climb on the porch roof and knock our landing window, directly opposite my bedroom. I'd get up, get dressed and out we'd go. Bike rides to Livingston Green, the journey there and back taking us forever; the day his brother, Charlie, took us to Cannock Chase, my mum worried sick because she thought Charlie wasn't the full shilling. I touch the scar on my forehead and smile – a trophy from the day Jack pushed me into his front door because I wouldn't share my biscuits.

I can't remember it raining when we shared the world. Sun, wind, ice, snow, but never rain. Everything happened outside. Kite flying, crossbows, bow and arrows, all home-made in my mum's back kitchen from pieces of wood, string, newspaper and old bits of elastic; British Bulldog, the last kid to try and make it across the green crushed by fifteen other kids tripping, punching, swearing, trying to inflict the greatest physical damage – if you were smart you got caught early. Hours and hours of just being kids. Marbles, conkers, swopping stickers – got, got, got – and, of course, every day we could, football.

Leeds United. I'd never been outside of Walsall, but they were my obsession. I still recall the team that won the 1972 FA Cup final, which Jack and I watched on a black-and-white TV in my mum's sitting room, trying to sort the aerial, to stop the picture rolling and four shadows of Mick Jones running up the pitch. When we played on the green, I became Alan "Sniffer" Clarke, a goal poacher, or Peter Lorimer, a toe punter. I remember Jack crossing the ball, Georgie Best style, and me scoring from a bicycle kick.

It all seemed idyllic, until it wasn't.

Seven years of age, Dad died, and I left the world, retreated inwards, became terrified of the dark – leave the light on, Mum. Leave the light on. It felt like I'd been sucked into a black hole, falling, falling, falling. My life stolen. I stopped going out, drifted around in Enid Blyton's Famous Five, talked non-stop to my teddies, missed months and months of school with a mystery back pain, lying on the settee, making safe worlds with my cowboys and Indians, occasionally venturing outside to chat with the clouds, which is where I thought Dad had gone.

Jack tried, but I wasn't there.

He called, knocked the landing window, his grubby face gurning at me, but I hid under the blankets, and he moved on, found another kid, Rob Cooper, to share his life.

I became a loner, a mummy's boy.

By the time I resurfaced, we were moving up the pseudo-social ladder.

My last memory of Jack is him and Rob Cooper visiting me in the new flat. They'd walked six miles to satisfy their curiosity. They knocked over all the potted plants in the communal area and called me a posh twat.

I write it all down.

My stomach is griping. I feel my tumour moving around, stretching out, poking its poison into my internal organs. It makes sense. It's alive. Curiosity must make it want to explore its new world. Perhaps I should let it. After all, I'm its host, and hosts need to entertain their guests.

My right hand starts to tremor.

Cancer grabs my gut.

I pick up the medicine pot, ready filled with ten mils of clear elixir, and gulp down the morphine. My face instinctively winces, always expecting bitterness, but it tastes of nothing, just slides down my throat, warming as it goes on its seek-and-find mission.

The hit registers in my brain.

I look out of the window.

At least the drizzle's stopped. Gives me a better chance of seeing some exotic birds through this pair of binoculars Claire, the home carer, gave me. 'It'll relieve the boredom,' she said. 'But no spying on the neighbours. I don't want any complaints about a Peeping Tom.' I bought a book, The A-Z of British Birds, but Passer domesticus, or the common house sparrow, is about as exotic as it gets. Still, what did I expect through a Walsall lounge window?

Birdwatching.

A council estate kid now a twitcher, checking out Latin names.

My buddy after Jack would have been impressed.

I put my hand on my stomach.

The morphine seems to have found its target.

I pick up my notebook.

Freddie.

Strange fish from very different ponds, but our worlds collided for a while in the 1970s. I blame Mum. She landed on her feet with the housing list after Dad died. 'You're lucky to get this,' said Roger from the neighbourhood office. 'They don't come up very often.'

Lucky. A shitty token gesture of three, three-storey blocks of council flats in a middle-class affluent suburb. Two bedrooms, rotting window frames, wallpaper sliding off the running-water-covered plaster, black mould sticking to my clothes, underfloor heating no one could use without robbing a bank to pay the bill. I lay in bed during the winter months, listening to Mum crying in the bathroom, her hands in hot water, trying to settle her ravaged arthritis. She tried to get a councillor on her side. Roger gave her a diary, a bottle of spray for the mould, told her to put on an extra jumper, to fill the holes in the frames with toilet tissue. She pushed her luck, went back. He gave her a dehumidifier, a fortune to run and useless against the tide of damp. 'You've moved up in the world, Mrs,' said Roger. 'Try and enjoy it.'

That's how Freddie and I came into the same orbit.

We went to Manor Farm Comp but never mixed there. His form had posh, nerdy kids who wore glasses, washed, had their clothes ironed, ticked the career officer's "this one has prospects" box; my form had the rest, the ones with nicknames like Tramp, the cocks of the school, the ones whose dads served at Her Majesty's pleasure. I clung like shitty pants to the third best fighter in our year, making me untouchable, out of everyone's reach, something that came back to bite me when I tried to return for sixth form, me exposed, but that's a different story.

My friendship with Freddie existed extra-curricular. He lived on a different planet, six bedrooms, opposite the golf course, municipal park-sized back garden, pull-on pull-off drive, radiators in every room, shower in the bathroom. His dad a company director who drove a Volvo estate, his mum a PA, holidays abroad every year, Malta, new trainers, leather bomber jacket, 501 jeans, season ticket holder at The Baggies.

I became his bit of rough.

At the end of each day, we got off the school bus at the last stop and headed for the newsagent. Cadbury's creme eggs for me, Express and Star paper for him. That's how we got talking, chatting on the wall by the OAP flats. Music, Yvonne Elliman for him, Elkie Brooks for me; TV, Dallas – who shot JR? Bobby's shower resurrection – Minder, That's Life, Rising Damp – he did a wonderful Leonard Rossiter impression, hands on hips, goofy grin, oh, Miss Jones.

Freddie's looks were more Kays Catalogue than street. His curtain hairstyle, long before David Beckham, held in place by copious resprays of Silvikrin. Roughing up his hair pissed him off, but he just pulled a comb out of his back pocket, found a mirror and reset it. Suddenly, girls who were way out of my league would shout at me in a plummy accent, "where's your mate?", "tell Freddie I said hello". He'd shrug when I told him and then tell me some football story.

He walked down most evenings from his oasis on the hill and sat in our flat, drinking tea and eating fondant fancies from Marks and Spencer, all served by my mum. He stayed over one night after we'd watched a Friday night Frankenstein film. We shared my single bed, sleeping top and tail. It never happened again. He said my feet stank.

We bunked off school, jumped on a bus to anywhere, nowhere, paid the minimum fare, camped out on the upstairs back seat, ignored the smell-cocktail of nicotine, piss and body odour soaking into the fabric, saw how far we could get before they kicked us off. Tamworth made us late home. The bus journeys stopped, but not the bunking off. We hid away in my mum's flat, him putting his feet up on our battered leather settee. The inevitable happened. His mum had a phone call from the school, turned up at the flat and drove us both to the headmaster. Two things I remember from that day: the school hadn't phoned my mum – I wasn't the one with prospects – and how incredibly sweet and polite Freddie's mum was, not shouting, staying calm, never telling my mum what had happened.

Kindness ran in his family. He helped my brother move house. We lay in the back of the empty removal van as my brother drove it, at speed, back to the hire company, our feet up on the sides, feeling every bump in the road, rolling with every turn, singing Racey's "Lay Your Love on Me" and Darts' "Come Back My Love".

Football dominated our time. Just the two of us, one-to-one combat in the nets, a sunken concrete park on the edge of the estate that you reached by walking down steps off the pavement. Freddie would stand one end of an area the size of a tennis court, me at the other, coats and jumpers setting out our individual goal behind us. You could score from a distance, but getting close up, tackling, chipping, swerving made it more likely. Losing the ball on the attack meant you were vulnerable, your own goal wide open. It went on for hours, only darkness bringing it to a close. In all the time we played, I don't remember seeing another person using the park. We had our own private playground, playing a game we'd designed ourselves.

A perfect existence, which soured in the adult world.

The end built up slowly, over weeks. The dole picked me up, queuing outside the labour exchange, clutching my

UB40, chatting to my mates from school, the ones who weren't in borstal. Freddie worked for his dad, meaning he could spend his days getting paid to restudy for his O levels, which we'd both failed. He joined the golf club, passed his driving test first time; his dad bought him a new yellow Datsun. I failed my driving test three times, passed on the fourth and, with the help of my mum, bought a rusted-up Morris Marina, which spent most of its mechanical failure life parked up kerbside outside our block of flats because I couldn't afford the petrol.

We still played football in the nets, but it became all I had. My head filled with his privilege, his leather jacket, training shoes, big house, golf, holidays abroad, new car, his moneybags dad. It knitted together, fuelling my rage. I kicked the ball harder, ran faster, fought for possession, tripped him up, demanded another game, and another and another. 'Calm down,' he said.

'It's you,' I said. 'You're getting soft in that office.'

He told me to piss off.

I ran over and punched him in the face.

I can still see the look he gave me as he held his nose, blood trickling through his fingers, like something in the world had fractured. I held up my hands and said sorry, but he shook his head and ran out of the park. Two days later, I walked up to his house. His mum answered the door, asked how I was, told me Freddie didn't want to see me, and then she said, 'Friendships do come to an end, you know.'

I didn't call again, and neither did he.

Friendships.

I write it all down.

Jack and Freddie.

We're sixty this year. I wonder where they are, what paths they travelled, what cards life dealt them. I hope they're okay. Stephen Hawking always talked about parallel universes where every moment in time continues to exist, being played over and over on a loop. I like to think that's true, that somewhere Freddie and I are still kicking a ball at each other in the nets, that Jack and I are still flying our kites. I suppose, looking back, the comfort is we found each other at all, that for a nanosecond of time our paths crossed.

I close the notebook.

Sleep drops my head forward, but I wake myself with a start. The notebook thuds as it hits the floor. I feel a flush rising up my body; sweat beads pop on my forehead. I reach towards the coffee table. Not yet. It's barely been twenty minutes since my last fix. A pinch in my stomach, a gentle prod. A reminder of my guest.

I look at the notebook.

No more writing. I can't do any more today.

The bus is back.

My neighbour, Ted, lands on the pavement, his hand in the air waving at me from the street. A distraction. He'll do. He talks. I listen. Tells me all about his holidays in the Maldives, shows me snap, after snap, after snap.

I force myself out of the chair and walk towards the front door.

I'll catch him on the landing if I'm lucky.

Locked In

A constant throbbing in my head, stiffness in my fingers, machines beeping, the white noise of a clunk, clunk, clunking respirator, waking up but not being awake. I'm punctured like a colander – stomach, throat, veins. Everything going in and out needs help. A tracheotomy blowhole in the front of my neck squirts phlegm.

Two nurses chatter over me. 'Do you think she can hear us?'

'They say she can, but she can't.'

'Her daughter sits for hours talking to her.'

'Fair play. Don't think I'd have the patience.'

'I heard the dad was some kind of war hero. Got himself killed.'

'Poor cow.'

They touch me, roll my carcass, scrunch a sheet against my back. Yank. Another roll. Yank. Another. It's over, except it isn't. They seize me by the shoulders, pull me forward, untie the gown at the back of my neck, slide it down my deadweight arms, drop me flat. I bounce slightly as my naked, paralysed body hits the mattress. A soapy flannel squelches against me.

No words.

A hard towel scrubs me dry; cold creams slap under my breasts; plastic gloves slip across my skin. They grab my shoulders, pull me up again; a new gown covers my bare flesh. A comb scrapes through my hair.

'That's her done.'

'Bloody good job. She gives me the creeps.'

'I know what you mean. It's like laying out a slab of sirloin every morning.'

The door slams.

I hear trolleys clattering in the corridor; the smell of antiseptic cloys. I try to move a part of me, anything. Nothing. Not even my eyelids. I crave for a stretch. The only view I have is inside my head, the only movement, a nanosecond blink in my big toe, which I repeat over and over. It's a start.

The door opens.

'Hello, Mum.'

Molly.

She squeezes my hand.

*

Molly sits at my bedside most days, talking about her childhood, me brush, brush, brushing her hair; the sailor's outfit I made her wear for a portrait picture when she was two, chubby legs squeezed by tight white socks, burgundy buckle shoes pinching her feet – 'You gave everybody a copy, Mum. It's so embarrassing,' – my bread-and-butter pudding, which she says I never told her how to make; the Christmas tree decorations we bought on holiday in the Isle of Wight; her fifth birthday when I lost her in St Ives and she headed for the beach, sat on the sand and stared at the sea while she waited for me. A fisherman asked her if he could buy her an ice cream. 'No, thank you,' she told him. 'My mummy will be here in a minute.'

I tell her how I spent hours watching her get grubby in the garden, climb the tallest trees, kick a football harder than the boys, talk about our pets – four cats, Charlie, Sophie, Boris and Tai – remind her how she dressed them up in ribbons, made them play house, tried to get them to sit at her pretend tea parties.

None of it reaches her.

The door opens again.

'She twitched, Doctor Kim. Just now, just before you came in.'

'You know it's just the muscles, Molly.'

I feel a squeeze on my hand.

'Oh God, Mum. What should I do?'

'There's no rush,' says the doctor. 'But it is a decision you have to make.'

'It's just, she looks like she's sleeping.'

'Your mum has gone, Molly.'

Molly cries. I want to put my arms around her, snuggle her into my body, stroke her hair, shush her tears away, buy her a pick-and-mix from Woolworths. 'I'm here,' I scream. 'I'm here. I'm here.'

I feel like a swede, a cauliflower, like I should be on a market stall waiting to be dropped into a brown paper bag. 'Come on, ladies, get your fresh veg here... that one's still covered in dirt, love. Pulled out of the ground this morning.'

I search my head, go inwards, free myself from this external cocoon.

*

I wander the streets.

I need to find him before it's too late.

'The blue one. Try the blue one.'

Molly runs up the conifer-lined driveway, fist bangs on the door, steps back, looks up at the windows, waits for a sign of life. 'There's no one here,' she shouts.

'There must be,' I say. 'Try again.'

She hits the door with two fists this time.

Nothing.

'He's gone, Mum. He's gone.'

'Next door, it must be next door.'

'I've already been there. It's none of them.'

'It is. It must be.'

'He's not there,' she says, falling to her knees. 'We've lost him.'

'No. He's here. We have to keep looking.'

We walk side by side down a jet-washed cobblestone road, pass a line of Victorian terraced houses, lush green lawns, neatly trimmed privets, garden borders of rhododendron bushes, aphid-free roses.

'This isn't right,' I say. 'He won't be here. This is where I grew up. Your dad didn't know these streets existed.'

'Where did you meet?' says Molly.

'What?'

'Perhaps you need to remember him, Mum, think about his life.'

'I was sunbathing in the park in my new cerise bikini. He leaned over the fence and asked if he could lend a tenner. I told him to bugger off.'

She smiles. 'Not the greatest chat-up line I've ever heard.'

'I can't believe I fell for it. Next thing I know he's walking me home. I blame the uniform, but his sleepy eyes and that cute little-boy-lost smile helped.'

'That's so sweet, Mum. Like Romeo and Juliet.'

'Not quite, darling. I was pregnant within a month. Three months later he was off to the South Atlantic.'

*

It's strange what the brain stores, brings to the surface when you have nothing else. Holding hands, being hugged, the warm body of another human being, the smell of eucalyptus, damp grass, white musk perfume, the taste of sea air, chilli, blue cheese, a runny boiled egg and soldiers, fish finger sandwiches.

Molly.

The thought of leaving her empties me, like someone syphoning away my blood.

A radio, Chris Evans' breakfast show, movement, two people at the foot of the bed.

'Matron told me they're going to switch off the machine tomorrow.'

'Not before time. They should have done it weeks ago.'

'She seems a bit calmer today, less twitchy.'

'Perhaps she knows.'

A clock ticks away from somewhere in the room.

*

I'm like an upside-down turtle, out of water, flapping about on my back, trapped by the anchor of my lifeless shell. Ahead of me is the ocean, the light blue of the shallow falling away at the coral reef into the dark blue of the deep. I can smell freedom, a swim away into the refreshing waters. All I need to do is find a way to get upright, to roll off my back.

Searching.

A voice screams at me to carry on looking. 'Find me. Find me. Find me.'

And there's something else, pricking away at my flesh, making it crawl, boiling my blood, making me want to crash my fist into someone's face. 'This is hopeless,' I say.

'You can't give up, Mum.'

'What if he's not here?'

'He is. Tell me about his childhood. Where did he live?'

I bring him back, the last time I saw him, waving him off at the train station, him dressed in full khaki, backpack thrown over his shoulders. Something burns in my stomach. I punch the ground.

'Mum,' says Molly. 'Are you okay?'

'He should be here,' I say.

'I know,' she says. 'And he is, somewhere.'

A new voice, a sickly, patronising voice grating away inside my head. I wretch, spit on the ground. It sounds like… it can't be.

'I can hear something,' I say, grabbing Molly's hand.

'Is it Dad? Have you found him?'

'Your granny's house. I only visited once.'

'Well?'

'It was so long ago.'

'Think. There must be something.'

'Yellow houses. I remember yellow houses.'

We cross over the road, turn another corner, walk towards a circle of 1950's steel-framed houses painted buttercup yellow, a play green with swings, a slide, makeshift goalposts in its centre, the smell of fish and chips and real coal fires.

The voice is stronger.

'This is it,' I say.

'Which house?'

'I can't remember.'

'We'll walk up and down until something clicks. Come on.'

We count down the numbers: forty-six… forty-four… forty-two…

I stop. 'It's that one,' I say. 'I recognise the red velvet curtains and the Murano glass dogs.'

'This is really weird,' says Molly.

'I know, sweetheart.'

'I love you, Mum.'

'I love you too,' I say, tears streaming down my face.

*

A fly lands on my nose during the night. I feel it walking about, investigating, buzzing. I panic that it might head up one of my nostrils, perhaps block my breathing tube. And then I relax, suck in the comfort of another heartbeat sharing my existence.

The sound of the church bells tells me another morning has arrived.

This must be what it's like on death row, except I don't get to enjoy a last meal, and I've done nothing wrong. A brain stem stroke. I never thought about my body and brain being in danger of disconnection, but that's what happened. No warning, no build-up.

The nurses are back, doing their final duty. They wash and change me, working around the pipework keeping me alive until my life switch can be flicked off. A stiff nylon sheet covers me, just my head on show. I feel a draught of breeze across my face from an open window, smell antiseptic wipes, hear birds singing a dawn chorus.

The door opens.

Footsteps head towards the bed.

My stomach churns.

They reach me.

'Are you ready, Molly?'

'Can you give me a minute, Doctor?'

'Not yet,' I scream. 'Not yet.'

*

We stand by the gate and look up at the house.

I draw in a deep breath, hug Molly again and walk up the driveway, gravel crunching underneath my feet. I reach the front door and single press the bell. The door swings open.

'What shall I do?' I say, looking back at Molly.

'Carry on, Mum. It's the only way you'll find out.'

I step inside, walk slowly down the hall, pass pictures of him, one in his sky-blue school uniform sat in the middle of his two sisters, doorstep photos in order of age, shoulder-length dark-black hair sticking out in all directions, the top two buttons of his shirt undone, a red check tie hanging loose in a wide knot, a black plastic bomber jacket, acne spots on his chin.

I open the lounge door.

He's sitting on his mum's brown leather settee, wearing his khaki uniform. Tears stream down my cheeks. I'm frozen to the spot. He stands up, opens his arms, smiles. I run over, hug him close, his Kouros aftershave taking me back thirty years. I pull away, hold his face in my hands, kiss him on the lips, over and over and over.

'Hello, my darling,' he says. 'I've been waiting for you.'

'Promise you'll never leave me again,' I say, slapping his arm. 'Promise. Say it now.'

'I promise,' he says, wiping the tears from his face. 'I promise.'

'Rejoice. Rejoice. Rejoice.'

I turn towards the sound.

A television, a still-frame flickering image of a British prime minister fills the screen. She's wearing a headscarf, sitting on top of a Chieftain tank, her voice on a repeat loop: 'Rejoice. Rejoice. Rejoice.'

'I don't understand,' I say.

'You needed something to guide you here,' he says. 'You needed me to be angry. It was the best I could find.'

'Oh, my darling,' I say, kissing him again. 'All those years. We've lost so much.'

He looks out of the window, towards the gate, towards Molly.

'I wish I could have held her,' he says.

*

I see an azure sky, falling away to infinity.

We're walking towards the horizon, hopping from cloud to cloud.

I feel Molly's breath and moist lips touch my face. 'Goodbye, Mum,' she whispers. 'Give my love to Dad.'

We burst into a run.

Pig

December 1936.

The King abdicates; divorce stigma spreads; and I'm married to a pig.

There he is, out cold on the lounge carpet, his cheek resting in a pool of puke.

I hear laughter from the street. Theresa's kids next door, back from the park, a house full of family. My rooms smell of stale whiskey. Pig made it stick to the plaster.

I kick him in the ribs, again and again and again.

He grunts.

'You're a stinking pig,' I say, grinding my stiletto into his hand. 'I hope you choke.'

Another grunt.

He lies there, gloopy vomit stuck in his hair.

I pick up my green suede handbag, fasten my mac, walk into the hall, open the front door and step out onto the pavement. A mist creeps around under the street lights. I get my leather gloves out of my pocket and pull them onto my hands.

'Evening, Mrs Hatley,' shouts Mr Truman from across the road.

'Evening,' I say.

'Saw your old man in the Maiden's Arms earlier. Did he make it home?'

'Oh, yes,' I say. 'He's upstairs, having a nap.'

'Glad he got back okay. Enjoy your evening.' He adjusts his hat, pulls up the collar on his overcoat and walks off towards the main road.

I slam my front door and follow him.

*

Live music night, a crowded church hall frilled up in Union Jack bunting, a big band filling the smoky air with trumpets, saxophones, trombones, a couple of guitar players, a piano and a double bass.

Art pulls me close, leans down and whispers in my ear, 'Tell me you're wearing those stockings I bought you,' he says.

I look him in the eyes. 'I might be,' I say.

He waltzes me around the floor; my cheeks flush; my heart races. The music stops. He grabs my hand and drags me towards the bar. 'Wait,' I say, pulling him to a standstill. 'Give a girl a chance to get her breath.'

He puts his hands on his hips. 'Well, if you can't take the pace.'

I slap his arm, pull a lace handkerchief from under the sleeve of my dress and dab at my brow. 'I'm sure you don't want me all sweaty.'

He smiles at me, and I slap him again.

'What?' he says.

'You know that's not what I meant.'

'Let me get you a drink,' he says. 'What is it? Another gin and pep?'

I nod and we walk over to the bar. Art finds two stools and a free table. I sit down and he pushes his way through the throng of people to get the drinks. 'If I'm not back in half an hour, send out the rescue dogs,' he says.

'Evening again, Mrs Hatley.'

I turn towards the sound of the voice. 'Mr Truman. I didn't know you liked dancing.'

'I don't, but they're a good band.'

'We do seem to have landed lucky. Your wife not with you?'

'Music gives her a migraine. I'm guessing it's not your old man's thing either.'

I shake my head. 'He's more of a pub man.'

'You managed to find a partner, though.'

I look at him, try to interpret the grin smeared across his face.

'Listen,' he says, running his hand through his Brylcreemed hair, 'call me Jimmy. Mr Truman sounds like I'm being interviewed by the police.'

'Jimmy,' I say.

He leans forward. 'And if you're ever short of company–'

'Here we are,' says Art, pushing through the crowd and thrusting a gin glass towards me. 'Luckily, I know the barman.'

I take the glass and nod towards the next table. 'My neighbour,' I say.

'Jimmy,' says Art, holding out his hand. 'Good to see you.'

'You know each other,' I say.

'We drink in the same pub,' says Jimmy. 'Sorry to hear about your wife, Art. How are those two little girls of yours?'

Art glances at me and then back at Jimmy. 'Well, you know, it's not been easy, but we get through. One day at a time as they say.'

'Did you sort a housekeeper?' says Jimmy. 'You were on the lookout last time we met.'

'I've had a couple since then,' says Art, taking a sip of his whisky. 'Bloody things are hard to keep.'

*

Art walks me home across the playing fields.

A cloudless sky, stars and planets winking down, a half-moon hanging overhead.

I shiver and snuggle into my mac.

He stops, takes me in his arms, kisses me, his handlebar moustache tickling my lips. He smells of soap. 'Let's sit down,' he says, nodding towards a park bench.

We sit.

He crosses his legs, takes my hand. 'Look, I should have mentioned the kids, but I didn't know how you'd react.'

'That's okay.'

'We have only seen each other a couple of times.'

'I said it's okay.'

'And you are married.'

'To a pig.'

'Even so…'

'I've told you what he's like.'

'He's still your husband, Em.'

I let go of his hand. 'Do you want to stop seeing me?'

'No, it's just, well, Jimmy's a bit of an old gossip. Your husband's bound to find out.'

'So what? He's done a lot worse.'

'Your reputation, though.'

'Listen, it's okay if you want to stop seeing me, but, if you do, you probably shouldn't be kissing me in a public park.'

'That's the problem,' he says, putting his hand on my leg. 'I can't help myself.'

He kisses me again.

*

Darkness.

No sound.

The light from a street lamp sneaks through a gap in the curtains, streaks across the carpet to illuminate his body.

I roll him onto his back, sit in the armchair, place a cushion on my lap, watch his chest rise and fall, rise and fall.

The cushion, smother him, a speedier way.

But they'd know; the post-mortem would know.

Best to let it happen. Watch it happen.

Wait for the vomit to heave into his mouth.

Rise and fall, rise and fall.

Whisky fuels his fists.

Punch, kick, slap.

Regret.

Flowers.

'It'll never happen again, Em.'

Until the next time, and the time after that, and the time after that.

Rise and fall, rise and fall.

A wait for change.

Nothing.

On and on he goes.

Rise and fall, rise and fall.

I scrunch the cushion and lean forward.

Heave. Please God, heave.

Rise and fall, rise and fall.

Art. A gentleman, a dancer, kind eyes, soft hands. Kids. I've never tried kids. Two girls. A ready-made family, waiting for a mum, waiting for a wife.

One heave. Do it now; do it now.

Rise and fall, rise and fall.

I put my hands together and pray.

*

Charlie, my solicitor, touches my arm. 'Are you okay?' he says. 'You seem miles away.'

'I just want to get it over with. I've been living with this for weeks now.'

'They won't get to you today.'

'I know, Charlie. The prosecution goes first. Puts their case for adultery.'

'You don't have to defend this, you know.'

'I want what I'm owed. That pig deserves to pay.'

He looks at his fob watch, which he keeps on a gold chain hanging out of the breast pocket of his pinstriped waistcoat. 'I think we should get in there,' he says.

I take a deep breath, stand up and walk behind him through the heavy door entrance to Courtroom Number One. Conversations stop, drop into hushed whispers; a stampede of eyes stare at me. The smell. Workday sweat mixed with musty wood, aged oak weighing everything down, a raised bench where the magistrates sit, the panelling in the walls, the tiered rows of seats, the boxing for the public gallery.

We sit on the front bench.

'Who are all these people?' I say.

'Mainly public and press,' says Charlie. 'Last night's newspaper didn't help. I'm assuming you saw it.' He drops the Observer clipping in my lap.

"An Unsavoury Case – Married woman, dancing, drinking, kissing men on park benches, husband heartbroken..."

'I read it last night. It makes me sound...'

'Ignore it,' says Charlie. 'Just keep looking at the bench and let me do my job.'

The courtroom door opens and in he walks.

Pig.

Rise and fall, rise and fall.

*

The magistrates. Three men sitting in front of a gold, red and blue royal coat of arms – an authority to dish out justice conferred from above. Their chair, Archer, has a long nose with thin, steel-framed glasses perched on the end. He looks like a bank manager.

'Order. Order.'

Jimmy takes the stand.

'You met Mrs Hatley at a dance,' says Pig's barrister.

'I did, sir.'

'Please tell us what you saw.'

'Her dancing with Art, making a play for him.'

'And this worried you?'

'It did. He's not long lost his wife to cancer.'

'You thought he was vulnerable.'

'That's right. That's why I told her old man.'

I wonder how many women Jimmy has for company when his wife isn't around, how many of them are married.

Charlie gets to his feet.

'So, you saw my client dancing at a dance. Is that correct?'

'Dancing with another man, yes.'

'And everyone else danced with their husband or wife?'

'Probably.'

'Come on, Mr Truman. A lot of people go to dances without their spouse. It doesn't mean anything, does it?'

'It's not right, not the way she carries on.'

'You were at the dance alone?'

'My wife had one of her heads.'

'But you always go alone, don't you?'

'Mostly. I like the music.'

'Do you drink?'

'Of course.'

'So you drink and go to dances alone. Are you making a play for other women?'

Laughter from the public gallery.

*

'Order. Order.'

Pig takes the stand.

He avoids my eyes.

I touch my ribs.

Pig's barrister goes first.

'Tell us about your marriage, Mr Hatley.'

'It was good, until she started playing around.'

'Other men, you mean.'

'I do, sir. Dancing, kissing and more. I've caught her on benches with them.'

'She carried on in public, did she?'

'She did, sir.'

'Read the paper,' shouts a woman from the back of the court. 'Tells you all you need to know.'

'Yeah,' shouts another woman. 'Poor man. She should be strung up.'

'Remove those two women,' says Archer.

A scuffle behind me.

I stare at Pig.

He takes a drink of water and meets my eyes.

'Dirty cow,' shouts one of the women.

'Slag,' shouts the other.

The courtroom door slams shut.

A smile twitches at the edge of Pig's mouth.

*

'Order. Order.'

The chilled silence smothers me like chainmail; the crowd's eyes drill into my back; reporters poise their sharpened pencils. Archer's gagged them for now, but the smears hover on their tongue tips – slag, cow, string her up; slag, cow, string her up.

Pig stands there smiling.

Charlie gets to his feet. 'That was quite a reaction, Mr Hatley. You must be pleased.'

Pig shrugs. 'It's not my fault what people think.'

'Isn't it? Haven't you been telling your story to anyone who'll listen?'

'It's the truth.'

'Have you been paid?'

'What?'

'By the press. Have they paid you money?'

'What's that got to do with anything? It's still true.'

'Tell me about your marriage,' says Charlie, looking down at his notes. 'Ten years. That's a long time.'

'We did alright.'

'And you were a good husband?'

'I never heard her complain.'

'Didn't you? What about your alcohol abuse?'

'I like a drink, but she put her fair share away.'

'And the beatings you gave her. Didn't she complain then?'

'What about me?' he says, holding up his bandaged hand. 'She can hold her own.'

I look up at the public gallery. Art. Best suit, front row, leaning forward, hands clasped together, staring at Pig, listening to every word. I wait for him to smile at me, but nothing.

*

It's over, for today.

'Get an early night,' says Charlie. 'It's your turn tomorrow.'

'All those things he said…'

'And tomorrow you can tell your side.'

'Why did they let him go on for so long?'

'Most of it was gossip. He had no evidence.'

'Most?'

'He did have that injury to his hand, and Truman's evidence about the dance helped him.'

'It wasn't like that…'

'And that's what we'll tell them tomorrow. Now, go home, and get an early night.'

He turns and walks off towards the stairs.

I open my bag, fetch out a tissue and blow my nose.

Art is standing outside the courtroom, Jimmy hovering at his side.

Pig is talking to both of them.

*

I watch the coal fire crackle away in the grate, blue flames firing up yellow plumes, roaring their force up the chimney.

Art hands me a mug of tea and sits down next to me. 'You must be exhausted,' he says.

I take a sip. 'I'll be glad when it's over.' I look up at him. 'Those people… what they said…'

'Forget them. They're gossips. They'll have read something else next week.'

'But the names they called me… you don't think…'

'We knew it would happen. As soon as we saw the article.'

His face falls into a frown.

I put my mug on the floor and squeeze his hand. 'That can't have been easy for you today.'

'No,' he says. 'The way he described your marriage… it sounded so, well, like you hated each other.'

'He's a pig.'

'Is it true what he said about his hand? Did you do that to him?'

'It was like a horror story, Art. He made me want to hurt him back.'

'You must have loved him once.'

'Maybe.'

'It scares me, Em. Two people who love each other ending up like that.'

'It happens. We were too young.'

'But you stayed.'

'I had no choice.'

'And now you do. Is that what I am? Your escape plan.'

I stand up. 'Is that what you think?'

'I don't know what to think.'

'I saw him talking to you. What did he say?'

'Nothing. He said nothing.'

*

The fire dies down to a few remaining embers, twinkling a dying light.

Art covers me in a blanket. 'Don't stay down here too long,' he says, kissing me on the forehead.

'I won't,' I say. 'I just need a bit of time to think, get ready for tomorrow.'

He leaves me on his settee, watching the fire go out.

Pig.

A smeared shit stain smile.

Rise and fall, rise and fall.

Slag, cow, string her up.

Filthy words of a pig.

I shiver as the last of the embers blink out of existence.

Art.

His face.

Disappointment.

It scares me, Em.

It scares me too.

I snuggle under the blanket.

Tomorrow.

Finale.

Pig.

Rise and fall, rise and fall.

*

Art and I arrive together.

Pig's barrister smiles as we reach the entrance to the courtroom.

Charlie joins us. 'How are you both feeling?'

'Nervous,' I say. 'But at least I get to talk today.'

Art says nothing. He's barely spoken all morning, still not told me what Pig said to him. I tell myself that's right and proper.

Two women whistle when I walk into court. I wonder if it's the same two as yesterday, who they are, what their lives are like. I take my seat. Charlie stands next to me.

'Order. Order.'

Art stands in the witness box, takes the oath, tells everyone how we met.

'And you knew Mrs Hatley was married?' says Charlie.

'I did, but we only danced and had a few drinks.'

'Nothing more.'

'No, sir.'

'I saw you snogging her,' shouts a man in the public gallery. 'You had your hand up her frock.'

Laughter.

Art looks at the floor, his cheeks flush.

'Remove that man,' says Archer.

'Oh, Christ,' says a woman behind me, 'here he goes again. You'll have to throw us all out soon.'

'And don't think I won't,' says Archer, nodding at one of the police officers who walks over and grabs the woman's arm.

'She's a tart,' says the woman as she's escorted out. 'Picking on decent men.'

The courtroom door slams again.

Art shakes his head in my direction. 'I'm sorry,' he mouths.

I give him a puzzled look.

'Continue,' says Archer.

'Just to confirm,' says Charlie. 'You danced and shared a few drinks. Nothing more.'

Art hesitates. 'We...'

'You danced and shared a few drinks,' repeats Charlie.

'No,' says Art. 'We kissed.'

*

A gentleman never lies.

I'm guessing those were Pig's words.

After that, it all comes out. How I'd moved into Art's house, become his housekeeper, shared his bed. The reporters scribbling away, struggling to keep up, creating tomorrow's headlines, the gallery gasping, gossiping in murmured voices.

Pig sits there grinning.

Charlie asks Archer if we can take a break.

We walk into the corridor.

'I'm sorry,' says Art. 'I tried, but I just couldn't…'

'It's okay,' I say. 'I should never have asked you to lie.'

'I'd advise you not to give evidence, Mrs Hatley,' says Charlie. 'And to drop your defence.'

'Yes,' says Art. 'Let's go home.'

I touch him on the cheek. 'You're a sweet man.'

'Nothing sweet about it. I need a housekeeper, and a wife.'

'I don't think I'm very good at either. Do you?'

'Then we'll work it out together.'

'I can't just walk away.'

'They'll slaughter you.'

'Maybe,' I say.

*

A toilet flushes.

The door in the cubicle next to mine opens.

I need to get back.

Fifteen minutes Archer said, and I've been sat in here for ten.

Slaughter. Today and tomorrow.

Squirm in the witness box, reporters salivating, or say nothing, skulk away in the shadows.

Art. Sweet, adorable, innocent.

Pig. His story, my life.

Rise and fall, rise and fall.

I flush the toilet, open the cubicle door, walk to the sink and wash my hands. My face in the mirror. Ten years of bruises, broken ribs, cigarette burns. For nothing. To watch him smirk and not have my say.

I dry my hands on the roller towel.

Plan B.

*

Art and Charlie smile as I walk towards them.

'You ready?' says Charlie.

I kiss Art on the lips. 'Thank you,' I say.

He looks embarrassed. 'What for?'

'For the kindness, and the fun.'

I turn and walk away from them.

'Em,' Art shouts. 'What's going on?'

I carry on walking.

There he is, chatting to his barrister, waiting for his triumph.

I put my hand in my mac pocket and squeeze the handle.

I take a deep breath, try to settle my heart rate, empty my head.

Pig sees me, smirks.

His barrister looks around. 'Mrs Hatley. You can't...'

I push the blade into Pig's chest, hit bone, pull it out, push it in again.

A soft spot.

Blood squirts down my arm.

Pig drops to his knees.

I lean down and whisper in his ear. 'That's my response,' I say.

Rise and fall, fall, fall...

Sea Boys

October 1943

A draught of ice air grabbed my breath as I dropped off the train.

I snuggled into my donkey jacket, pulled my woollen scarf up under my chin and looked along the wind tunnel platform.

A crowd of boys spilled out of the carriages, my age, sixteen, spotty faces, fresh from their mammy's skirts, trying to look tough, in control.

'This is it then,' said Billy, a short-arsed, six stone wringing wet lad from Birmingham. 'No going back now.'

'Looks like it,' I said.

'Over here,' shouted a man in a Merchant Navy uniform, a badge on his blue-black cap showing a union jack and red duster. He held up a clipboard, and we all walked over and gathered around him.

I stood at the back of the group, smoking my fag, blowing smoke towards the station's tin roof, Billy hovering at my side.

'My name's Strange,' said the man. 'I've heard all the jokes, so don't bother. Let's see who had the balls to get this far.' He ticked off our names on his clipboard sheet.

'Jackson, Perry, Chilton, Marshall, Bretherton…'

'Brotherton,' I corrected him, taking a last drag of my fag before throwing it to the ground and stamping the nub end into the paving stone.

'Right,' he said, ticking the box. He limped over. 'You got any more of those?' he said, nodding at the squashed butt.

I reached into my jacket and pulled out a pack of Park Drive.

He took two and grinned. 'You're a tough guy, aren't you?' he said.

'Not really,' I said, dropping the fags back into my pocket.

'Not really, sir,' he said, pushing his stale beer breath into my face.

'Not really, sir,' I repeated.

'Not so hard, is it?' he said, lighting the fag, taking a drag and puffing smoke into my eyes.

I stared him out, forcing myself not to blink.

He smiled, faced the group and finished his roll call. With a swish of his pen, he put the last tick in place, jammed the clipboard under his arm and clicked his heels together. 'Follow me,' he said, 'and try not to look like the slobs you are.'

Petty Officer Strange, the bosun. I found out later he'd spent two weeks in a lifeboat, his ship sunk by a Russian convoy. Frostbite had gnawed his toes and, to save his life, a steward had chopped them off with an axe.

Strange marched us along a road for three miles, over the River Severn bridge, ice crunching underneath our feet, down onto a towpath, to the docks. We stopped at the sight of an old hulk ship, its masts removed, looming at us out of the fog. 'There she is, boys,' said Strange. 'Your home for the next twelve weeks.'

'Bloody hell,' said Billy. 'She's massive.'

'Last chance,' said Strange. 'Once you're on board the navy owns you, and you belong to me.'

I strode up the gangplank, feeling it bounce beneath me.

The rest of the lads followed.

*

And so it began.

The ship became everything.

Bugle calls at sunrise and lights out regulated the day.

We ate in the mess and slept in bunk beds on the bottom deck. I nipped in quick and grabbed a top berth, telling Billy, who seemed to have decided we were mates, 'I don't want you farting in my face all night.' He said he preferred being closer to the ground, not so far to fall if he rolled out.

Our group divided into two squads, alternating every morning between cleaning duties – rubbing up the brasses, scrubbing the decks, emptying the sewage bin, galley work – and exercising – sit-ups, push-ups, knee bends, running backwards and forwards to the River Severn bridge, an officer poking you with a branch to keep you moving.

It took a while to get used to forcing down the food. The first couple of days most of us left something, the more experienced lads wolfing the grub before we changed our minds. Stale bread pasted with dripping; mugs of tepid cocoa brewed in large steel vats and diluted with bromide to quench your libido; seafood pie seasoned with cockroaches; tales from the galley lads of baby mice falling out of their nest into the stewing pot, the cook giving them an extra stir to make sure they were well hidden. Refusal meant starvation, the meagre rations barely enough to fuel the workhorse graft of a full day on ship.

Strange haunted everywhere, appearing at my side like a ghost. Rumour had it that on a full moon he rode around the deck naked on a vicar's bike, howling at the sky. His party piece used to be walking up behind you at mealtime, grabbing an earlobe, twisting it and whispering, 'Go home, son. You're not fit to wear the uniform.' Billy used to get it a lot, and he screamed like a baby every time, the whole mess deck laughing when it happened, Strange beaming at the reaction, sucking in the response from everyone.

'You should bite your lip,' I told Billy. 'Don't let him win.'

'It's alright for you,' he said. 'You can look after yourself.'

There were plenty of other lunatics to keep Strange company.

Lewis, the cook, aka Popeye, who used to blow his cheeks out like a balloon, go blood red in the face and shout in a pirate's voice, 'Where's me Olive gone?'; Nurse Grey, aka Codeine Annie, who dished out painkillers like smarties for every illness known to man; Agate, the PT instructor, aka Squirty, who toured the bunk deck every morning with a squeezy bottle filled with cold water, squirting anyone who didn't respond instantaneously to the bugle. He arranged boxing matches on deck, pairing off weedy, nerdy kids with proper bruisers and salivating ringside as he watched the inevitable beating.

An asylum with inmates in charge.

By Friday of the first week, half the squad had crawled out of the bed deck portholes in the middle of the night, over a pontoon to the shore and legged it to the station, catching the next train home. I thought about it, but they'd taken my ration book and my mum couldn't afford to feed me.

*

Look after your squad.

The ship's mantra.

One of the lads, Johnny, made a fortune with his penny anchor thumbprint Indian ink tattoos. He said if we ever met up again in life, we'd know a fellow sea boy by his thumbs-up hello. Camaraderie. The instructors loved it, but it didn't stop the gangs seeking out and preying on anyone who showed weakness.

Billy missed his mum, used to call for her in his sleep. I'd throw a shoe at him to wake him up, conscious the other lads could hear him. He followed me everywhere, became my shadow. Luckily, we were in the same squad, but, occasionally, we got split up. One day, a Geordie lad called Cheetham and a few of his cronies got hold of Billy in the bogs, a couple of them pinning him to the floor while Cheetham pissed all over him. 'Tell your girlfriend we said hello,' said Cheetham. Billy told me that night, in-between gasps of struggling breath, 'You know what he's saying; he thinks we're queer.'

I waited until lights out, walked down the deck, dragged Cheetham out of his bed and stamped on his head. His nose split in two. I pulled him up to my face, feeling the stares from the surrounding bunks. 'Call me queer again,' I said, 'and I'll do you.'

He spent the rest of the week in sickbay, Codeine Annie tending his wounds.

To his credit, Cheetham told Strange he'd slipped on deck, but I knew it wasn't over. 'Listen,' I said to Billy. 'You need to toughen up. I can't be there all the time to look after you.'

'Or leave,' he said. 'I might just jack it in.'

'Is that what you want?'

'It'd kill me dad,' he said, shaking his head.

'We'll think of something,' I said. 'Stay by me as much as you can, and keep out of Cheetham's way.'

*

I lived for Saturday shore leave, but it could be taken away at the drop of a hat. Talking after lights out, failing deck inspection, fighting outside the ring. These were the big no-nos. One breach and the whole squad suffered. 'Don't fuck up our leave.' Everyone understood the rule, and doing something stupid, that you should have avoided, could get you a group kicking if you couldn't hold your own. I think that's why Cheetham lied about his nose, that and to save face.

Getting off the ship meant I escaped the madness, but I became a bit of a loner on these trips. Billy stayed onboard most of the time. He told me he felt like a fish out of water in the big wide world.

Most of us went to the Seaman's Mission as a first stop, suffering the out-of-tune piano playing for sandwiches, a bun, a cup of tea and, on good days, jam or beans on toast. Heaven after Popeye's gut-stirring offerings. After that we moved on to do our own thing.

The pictures in Berkley became my big draw, led to my seat by an usherette with a torch, lighting up my fag, suffering the Donald Duck and Mickey Mouse cartoons, waiting for my silver screen goddess: Betty Grable.

I sat open-mouthed, cigarette long forgotten, her legs filling the screen, hot pants, high heels, boxing gloves, dancing with a shadow – two Betty's for the price of one. In my foggy mind, she performed "I Heard the Birdies Sing", just for me, sending me a seductive wink halfway through the number. I had a poster of her on my wall back home, her in a bathing suit, bare back to the camera, an iconic over the shoulder pose. Years later, I found out she posed in that way because she was visibly pregnant at the time. It didn't matter. Betty Grable. My route out of mundanity. A way of keeping my sanity.

The curtain fell.

I headed outside, shaking my head to get back in the world, blinking my eyes at the light as I came into the foyer.

And that's when I saw her.

My own real-life goddess.

*

Second night on ship, Strange warned us off the local girls. 'Career in the navy ahead of you, you're their passport out of this shithole. Keep it in your trousers, or they'll eat you alive.'

She had brunette, peekaboo-style hair and wore a calf-length, polka-dot dress with matching red pixie boots.

I asked her name.

'Maggie,' she said.

Her two friends giggled, made their excuses and left.

I watched them walk out into the street.

'We're not allowed to talk to you sea boys,' said Maggie.

I ran my fingers through my buzz cut hair. 'A bit of a giveaway, I suppose.'

'And the way you walk. Like you're a somebody.'

'How come you're still here then?' I said, feeling a flush of irritation.

She shrugged. 'I'm thinking about it,' she said. 'Buy me an ice cream, and I'll tell you if I'm going to ignore my dad's pearls of wisdom.'

I gave her a puzzled look.

'Just sitting on a bench with you might get me pregnant,' she said.

'Sounds like good advice,' I said. 'Perhaps an ice cream might protect you.'

*

We spent the next three Saturdays walking along the canal towpaths, her telling me about her dad's dairy farm, her favourite cows, Mable and Midge, how she had to get up at 5am every morning to help with the milking and ride the milk cart into town. I told her about Middlesbrough, sharing a room with my twin sisters, Floss and Jess, Dad dying in a mining collapse. 'Thirty-two,' I said. 'It killed Mum.'

'You sound lonely,' said Maggie, touching my face.

'You can't be lonely on a boat full of sailors,' I said, looking at the ground, trying to stop my cheeks from blushing.

'Yes, you can,' she said, lifting my head and kissing me on the lips.

I could taste her sticky cherry red lipstick and smell the powder from her cheeks, some of which had rubbed off onto my donkey jacket. 'Now that,' I said, brushing the hair out of her eyes, 'is much more dangerous than sitting on a bench.'

'Lucky I've had my ice cream then. Anyway, you've already been unfaithful.'

'I wouldn't,' I said. 'Who with?'

'Miss Grable. I bet you think about her every night when you're in bed.'

'Ah, well, that's, she's got…'

'What?'

'I'm not sure I should say.'

'Tell me or I'll scratch your eyes out.'

'It's just, I've seen her legs and, to be honest, well, they're insured for a million dollars.'

Maggie looked down at her boots, pinched the hem of her dress and lifted it above her knees. 'Small change. That's as much as a million dollars gets you from me.'

I grabbed her hand, dragged her off the path and pulled her into my body. The winter sun found us through the tree canopies and stroked the top of my head.

A duck honked from the canal.

'I think your dad might have found us,' I said.

*

We lay on our stomachs, draped our hands in the canal water and stirred, making ripple after ripple after ripple. 'Mine's the biggest,' said Maggie, a piece of straw hanging from her mouth.

'So it is,' I said, putting my arm around her shoulders.

I looked at the water; my gaunt reflection stared back at me. For some reason, surrounded by all the others on the ship, I hadn't noticed the weight loss, but here, in the real world… 'Do you think I look ill?' I said.

'A bit,' said Maggie. 'I don't think they feed you enough.'

'Trust me,' I said, 'you don't want too much of Popeye's cooking inside you.'

I looked again at the water, our mirrored faces side by side on the surface.

'What are you thinking?' said Maggie.

'I'm just wondering about the future,' I said.

'You'll finish on that boat soon. I'm guessing you'll be off to sea then.'

'And what about us?'

'You'll soon get your girl in every port.'

'And you'll move on, find another sailor.'

She stood up and walked away down the towpath.

I jumped up, ran after her and grabbed her arm. 'I'm sorry. I didn't mean–'

'If you must know,' she said, facing me, tears rolling down her cheeks, 'you're the first and last.'

I reached into my pocket, pulled out a folded-up white handkerchief and wiped her face.

'How can you think that of me?' she said, taking my handkerchief and blowing her nose. 'And yes, you do look ill, and I worry about them not feeding you on that boat, and I'll probably spend the rest of the war wondering where the hell you are, who you're with, if you've been blown up collecting sugar from God knows where in the world or whatever it is you do...'

I put my finger on her lips. 'I love you,' I said.

'What?'

'I said, I love you.'

'You can't say things like that unless you mean it.'

'I mean it,' I said.

She blew her nose again and held the handkerchief out to me.

'Keep it,' I said. 'Your need is greater than mine.'

She hugged me. 'I love you too,' she whispered.

*

Back on board, the madness deepened.

I found a bit of peace through my turn on nightly fire watch, sneaking a sit-down, my legs dangling over the ship's side, looking out at the moonlit water, puffing away on my Park Drive, listening to the vessels in the dock tugging at their moorings, thinking about Maggie. I even got used to the cockroaches, which, by the light of an oil-lamp, you could see carpeting the deck, a black mass writhing and wriggling over and underneath each other.

The instructors added classes to our day – how to box the compass, reciting the thirty-two points in order; how to splice one-inch steel cables; how to read a map; how to stow gear in a lifeboat.

Boys Own bullshit.

Join the navy, see the world, do your bit; the reality of forced conscription, poverty-ridden cannon fodder, a likely fate of being blown up by a U-boat, screaming until you died in an oil tanker fire. Not such a good poster. Much better to believe the, your country needs you, chat-up line, make Daddy proud.

No choice if I wanted to flee the shithole slums of Middlesbrough.

Keep your head down. Go to sea. Escape the rat trap.

I distracted myself with Agate's boxing tournament, adopted Jake LaMotta's bullying style, going in low, sweat spraying, absorbing my opponent's punches, staying close, looking for a chance of landing a knockout blow. A raging bull. Earlier in the year, I'd listened on the radio to LaMotta's fight with Sugar Ray Robinson, the eighth round, LaMotta landing a right to Robinson's head, a left to his body, pummelling him for the rest of the fight, winning by unanimous decision, the immortal Robinson's first defeat.

I made it through to the final without losing a round.

Cheetham scraped through his semi on a points decision.

It stank of a fix.

He'd grown in popularity, fed by his cigarette laundering through an onshore supplier. Him and his cronies haunted Billy, dished out proper beatings at least once a week. Billy lifted his shirt and showed me the black and purple bruises across his ribcage. 'They threatened to hang me from the ship's figurehead,' he said. 'It was only Popeye coming on deck that stopped them.'

'You've got to protect yourself.'

'I'm useless without you. It's worse on a Saturday when you're not here.'

'I can't be here all the time, Billy.'

'I don't know what to do,' he said.

'It'd do you good to get on shore for a bit. Perhaps you need to tell Strange about these guys.'

'He's worse than them. You know that. You need to talk to Cheetham, offer him something, get him to stop.'

'The only thing he understands is a punch in the mouth,' I said.

'He's desperate to win that fight,' said Billy.

*

I found Cheetham sitting cross-legged on a lower bunk, dealing out cards to three of his gang, who were kneeling at the side of the bed. 'Twist. Twist. Twist. Shit. I'm bust.'

Doughnut, an acne-scarred kid from Bristol, threw his cards on the mattress.

'What do you expect, you fat fucker?' said Cheetham. 'Thirty-two. You were bust before you had that last card.'

The other two lads laughed and pushed Doughnut to the floor.

'Hang on, lads,' said Cheetham, seeing me at the end of the bed. 'We've got company.'

He turned off the bunk, stood up and faced me.

'Can I have a word?' I said.

'You can have two,' said Cheetham. 'Piss off.'

'It's about the fight,' I said.

'Go on. I'm listening.'

I looked at the others, who were now on their feet behind their leader. 'In private,' I said.

'Give us a minute, boys,' said Cheetham.

'Perhaps he wants to join us,' said Doughnut.

Cheetham grabbed Doughnut's arm and threw him against the bedframe. 'I said, fuck off.'

All three of them slunk away, heads bowed.

'Big and brave, aren't they?' I said.

'They do what they're told. You still hanging around with that thin streak of piss?'

'Billy,' I said. 'I hear you've been seeing a lot of him as well.'

'It passes the time, and I know it winds you up.'

'I want you to leave him alone.'

'Or what, tough guy? You going to fight all of us for him?'

'No. I'm going to give you something.'

He gave me a puzzled look. 'You mean the fight. You'd do that for him.'

'I want your word he won't be touched.'

'I don't need you to throw a fight. I intend beating the crap out of you.'

I stepped forward and grabbed his face. 'I'll give you the fight, you'll leave Billy alone. If you don't, I'll put you in hospital, shitting in a pot and drinking through a straw for the rest of your life.'

He tried to pull my hand away, but I gripped his skin harder. 'Give me your word,' I said.

'Okay,' he said. 'You have my word.'

I let go of him.

He sat down on the bed. 'You'd better make it look good. Strange is no fool.'

'All you need to do is stay on your feet for three rounds and land a punch on me in the fourth.'

'I can't believe you'd do that for the weedy kid.'

'No,' I said. 'Neither can I.'

*

I laid my head in Maggie's lap and looked up at the clouds. 'Do you know,' I said, 'no cloud formation is ever the same. What we're seeing up there now will never be like that again. It's unique to us. Like a fingerprint.'

She looked up at the sky. 'Is that true?' she said.

'Probably,' I said. 'That's what some of the artists reckon.'

She stroked my hair and touched the bruise underneath my right eye. 'Are you okay? I hope Billy realises what you did for him.'

'It's only a fight. Cheetham will leave him alone now.'

'What if he doesn't?'

'I'll deal with that if it happens.'

She turned her legs from under me.

I sat up. 'What's wrong?'

'All this fighting. It sounds like, well, it sounds like it's never going to end.'

'You can't let people like Cheetham win, Maggie.'

'It's not just Cheetham, is it? This bloody war is going on forever, and you'll, I don't know, you can't fight everyone's battles. What else can you do?'

'I won't need to do anything else.'

'I hope you're right,' she said. 'I don't want to lose you.'

*

I could hear the commotion from the gangplank as I boarded.

Popeye's voice bellowed orders. 'Get him down. That's right. Careful.'

I raced up to the deck.

Four oil-lamps. Elongated shadows, most of the boys watching, even though it must have been getting close to lights out. Cheetham stood next to Doughnut, both of them with their hands tied behind their back. Agate stood behind them.

Two of the new recruits lifted the stretcher holding Billy's body. I could see a rope thrown on the side, the noose still tied but slackened. He looked up at me and smiled as they carried him past. I reached out and touched his outstretched hand.

Strange dropped his arm around my shoulder. 'He's alive,' he said. 'And they're under arrest.'

'I'll kill him,' I said. 'He gave me his word.'

Agate pushed Cheetham and Doughnut in the back. They followed the stretcher towards the gangplank. I went to move forward, my fists clenched, but Strange held me back. 'Calm down,' he said.

'Is Billy okay?' I said.

'He's shook up, but he'll be fine.'

'I suppose you're happy now.'

'Happy?'

'Yeah, happy. I wouldn't be surprised if you arranged it.'

'I'll ignore that,' he said. 'I'll make allowances because you're upset.'

He turned and went to walk away.

I ran round and stood in front of him. 'You're a coward, sir. A bully and a coward.'

Strange looked around the deck.

Everyone had their eyes on us, even Popeye.

My stomach churned; tears welled in my eyes; sweat popped on my brow. My fists clenched even tighter at my side, my nails digging into the palms of my hands. One punch. I knew he'd go down if I hit him, hit anyone.

'And you think you're able to judge that, do you? You're sixteen. What do you know?'

'I know a bully when I see one. What chance did Billy have with you as his protector?'

'More than he had when he started here. Toughening him up. That's my job. Better he learns it here than when he's got a U-boat up his arse.'

'He's not capable of looking after himself.'

'Then he needs to find another job.'

That's when I should have thrown my arm, banged a punch into his face, raging bull style, but Maggie dropped into my head. I slackened my fists.

Strange turned away and clicked his boots together. 'Lights out in five minutes,' he said. 'Anyone still out of his bunk will be disciplined. Now, stop bloody gawping and get to bed.'

With that, the deck emptied.

'That goes for you as well, son,' said Strange, facing me.

*

I stared up at the wooden ceiling, the bunk bed below me empty.

Moments in time.

Crossroad decisions, left or right.

Sixteen. I'd only left school a year ago. Mum, my sisters, they needed me to do something, to be the man, to do my bit. And then I'd met Maggie, my goddess, who stroked my hair, listened to my ramblings about clouds and didn't want any more fighting.

We'd eaten at Maggie's earlier, tin mugs of tea, homemade cake, her dad squeezing her mum's shoulders and holding her hand, her little brother staring at me as he bit a chunk out of his paste sandwich. 'Are you Mag's boyfriend?' he said, sniggering into his bread. Maggie told him not to talk with his mouth full, her face florid with embarrassment.

Maggie.

Family.

I threw back the blanket, rolled out of bed, got dressed, pushed my clothes into my kit bag, tiptoed along the deck, carrying my boots, opened one of the portholes and climbed out.

Dancing with Dad

I first noticed the thing between Dad and my big sister, Emma, when I got home early from school, went to the sink to get a glass of water and saw them through the kitchen window.

They were playing swing.

Dad pushed her higher and higher.

She squealed louder and louder. 'Stop it, Dad,' she shouted. 'Stop it.'

He moved to the front of the swing and held out his arms. 'Jump, my darling. Jump.'

Emma shook her head and laughed as the swing went back up.

'Jump,' he said again.

She let go and two seconds later he caught her, sliding her slowly to the floor.

He kissed her forehead. 'Well done,' he said. 'My big, brave girl.'

'That was great, Dad. Can we do it again?'

'Of course we can, sweetheart.'

I ran outside, wiping my hands on my dress. 'Can I have a go, Dad?' I said.

'After me,' said Emma, running back to the swing. 'I want to go higher this time.'

'Perhaps later,' said Dad. 'You both need to get ready for tea.'

He walked into the house.

Emma glared at me. 'Why do you have to spoil everything?' she said.

*

I watched them closely after that.

'She's getting too big,' I'd tell myself.

And then Tina, my little sister, had her seventh birthday party.

I walked into the front room and there she was, the baby, sitting on his lap. 'Take a big breath, our Tina, and blow out your candles,' said Dad.

She blew spit all over the cake.

I waited for him to scold her, but he tousled her hair and tickled her until she giggled. 'You're my favourite,' he said. 'You're my special girl.'

Emma gave me a strange look.

Mum stared at the floor.

I went and sat on the bottom step of the stairs.

Mum came and sat next to me.

I buried my face in her housecoat. She smelt of Pledge and Fairy Liquid. 'Why doesn't he love me, Mum?' I said.

'I love you,' she said, squeezing me and making a shushing noise.

*

The next day, Emma went off for a sleepover at her friend's

house, and I went shopping with Mum. 'You deserve a treat,' said Mum. 'Let's go and get that Cindy you're always going on about.'

Dad wanted to watch the cup final on telly, and he stayed at home with Tina.

We went to Woolworths to get the doll, the one with Cindy dressed in a pink ballerina skirt. 'You need to look after her,' said Mum. 'We'll buy her some more outfits.'

'I will, Mum,' I said. 'I will.'

After I'd finished my 99 ice cream, Mum got one of her headaches, and we came back early. 'We're back, Joe,' she shouted, throwing the carrier bags on the hall floor.

A floorboard creaked in the spare room.

'They're upstairs,' I said, walking up a few steps.

Dad appeared on the landing. He wasn't wearing his tie, and the top three buttons of his shirt were undone. I could see his grey chest hairs and the start of his anchor tattoo.

'Hello, love,' he said. 'I didn't expect you back so soon.'

Mum looked at me. 'Come on,' she said. 'Let's get the tea started.'

'What about Tina?' I said. 'I want to show her my Cindy.'

'I'll bring Tina down,' said Dad.

Mum put her arm around me, and we walked down the hall and into the kitchen.

*

A few weeks before Tina's party, we were at my cousin Tanya's wedding.

Spandau Ballet's "True" started up, and Dad walked across the dance floor towards me.

He put his arm around my waist and waltzed me around the room.

'You're so headstrong,' he whispered. 'Why can't you be more like your sisters?'

'I can, Dad.'

I could smell his tangy Aramis aftershave as he spun me faster and faster. I had to concentrate really hard to keep up with him. Don't let him down, I kept telling myself. I couldn't see Mum, but I knew she was watching, and our Emma, and our Tina.

And then he stopped dancing and held me at arm's length. 'You're no good at keeping secrets, Becky,' he said. 'I could never trust you.'

'I am, Dad. I am.'

He walked away in the direction of the bar.

Mum came over and hugged me.

'What does he mean, Mum?' I said. 'I can keep secrets.'

'It's not you, sweetheart,' she said. 'There's nothing wrong with any of you.'

I spent the rest of the night trying to work it out, watching him drinking beer with my uncles, everyone patting him on the back and laughing at his jokes. Mum never left my side, kept kissing the top of my head. 'We'll go shopping again on Saturday,' she said. 'Just you and me.'

Guilt Trip

A cold, wet potato fills my palm. I squeeze, but it cannot be crushed, not yet, not until it's been boiled within an inch of its life. I hear my mum's voice in my head, *scrape not peel. You'll get more for your money that way.* Spuds served her well, her yellow handle, stainless steel saucepan overflowing, Saxa salt and knobs of butter chucked in to add flavour, mash piled high on dinner plates, covered in Oxo gravy. *Get it down you. It'll do you good.*

Mum. Her life spent in a housecoat.

I peel, set myself a challenge to uncover in one ringlet.

The hours I've spent at this kitchen sink, getting his tea ready, in plenty of time to settle down for the news, his conifers my only view. Flowers. That's what I need. Hack all his trees down, load the borders with topsoil, get some colour. Roses. They were my mum's favourite.

Horse shit. Roses need horse shit.

I throw the knife onto the draining board; drips of blood splash into the Belfast sink, stream down the plughole under the force of the running cold-water tap.

'Are you okay?'

'I'm fine.'

'Let me see.'

'It's nothing,' I say, sucking the end of my finger.
'I want to meet him.'
'That's not going to happen.'
'How long?'
'Tony, please, I've told you everything.'
'How long were you seeing him?'
Silence.
'We'll go today.'
'What's the point? It's over. I'm not going.'

*

I fix my eyes on the shimmering tail lights of a Ford Capri, concentrate hard, apply more and more pressure to the accelerator. A lorry screams past in the opposite direction and throws up a splash of water, triggering the automatic wipers to shift into frenzy mode and block out the world. A blurred bus stop queue races by, people waiting stoically for the number forty-nine, umbrellas drawn against the downpour.

'Was he better than me?'
'Why are you making me do this?' I say.
'You know why.'
Silence.
'I said–'
'I heard you.'
'Then why aren't you answering me?'

'Jesus,' I scream, slamming my foot on the brake pedal, skidding the car to a halt. The engine stalls; honking horns sound all around. I thump the steering wheel. 'Please can we go home?'

'I want to see him.'

'You know I love you.'

'I need to see him.'

*

I pull into the gravel driveway and yank hard on the handbrake, the rain bouncing off the car roof. I turn towards the passenger seat. 'I was coming back to you,' I say. 'Why don't you believe me?'

Silence.

I look at the house. 'I can't do this.'

'You have no choice.'

I step out into the storm, pull my hoodless anorak tight and crunch up the path. The security light spots my presence, lights me up, shames me out of the shadows. Disco nights, Bacardi and coke, Japan, Human League. Blink. Twenty-five years of marriage pass; he turns into a pot-bellied, catatonic, telly-watching drudge, and a new romantic catches my eye.

I reach the front door and hesitate.

'Ring it. Ring it now.'

I press the bell, rain dripping off my face.

The house stays in darkness.

'There's no one home,' I say.

'Try again.'

Hesitation.

Another ring.

The hallway light comes on.

My stomach drops.

The door opens.

'Good God, Helen, you're soaked…'

'It's Tony,' I say.

'Tony?'

'He's here, Gary.'

'Come inside,' he says. 'You'll catch your death.'

'You mustn't touch me. He's watching.'

'What's going on?'

'Tell him. Please tell him.'

He pulls me to his chest, kisses the top of my head. 'Tony's dead, sweetheart.'

I push him away. 'Don't say that. You must tell him.'

'I don't understand.'

'That I was going back to him. The night of his car crash.'

He hugs me close. 'You were never going back, my darling. Let's get you some dry clothes.'

'No,' I say, looking at the empty car. 'You must tell him I was going home.'

A New Beginning

Open your eyes, Grace. Open your eyes.

Dead.

So final, but nothing ever truly starts or ends.

A tiny oak coffin, a horse-drawn hearse, me collapsing at the graveside.

Ethan.

Mummy's little soldier shot down by leukaemia.

Ten years.

I need more.

The end of one thing must by definition be the start of something new.

That must be right.

I remember the platform, the train, the leap, but my senses live.

An aroma of menthol tickles my nasal passages; my dry tongue pushes around my mouth in search of moisture; my fingers press into the slightly damp ground beneath me; heat warms my face; and I can hear the voice.

Open your eyes, Grace. Open your eyes.

I want to obey, but I feel afraid, unsure of what awaits me. That's silly, I tell myself. You can't spend the rest of eternity with your eyes shut.

You're safe, Grace. It's time to wake up.

A woman, softly spoken, no accent. She keeps using my name, trying to bond, gain my trust. It might be a trap. But this is what I want. Life after death. Whatever that means. Heaven. Hell. Plato's souls racing out of the shadows at Olympic-sprinter speed back to the perfect cave. Buddhism's infinite cycle of rebirth until Nirvana.

I don't care what it is as long as I'm alive.

It all boils down to the same thing.

We can be together again.

That's right, Grace. He's waiting for you.

'I'm coming, my darling,' I whisper. 'I'm coming.'

I open my eyes.

*

I'm lying on grass, surrounded by trees.

Beams from the sun pick me out like an actor caught in spotlight.

I push myself up on my elbows and look around.

'Okay,' I say. 'My eyes are open. Where are you?'

'I'm here,' says the voice.

A woman walks towards me.

She's wearing a blue pinstriped suit and red pixie boots.

'You're not what I expected,' I say.

'You thought an angel with wings. Is that right?'

'Something like that.'

'Are you disappointed?'

'Not if you can find him.'

She turns and points towards the wood. 'Follow me,' she says.

*

Night falls.

A full moon reflects off a rippling lake; legions of pond hoppers skate across fresh green lily palms; a swarm of mosquitoes hover at the reedy banks.

'We must keep moving,' she says, putting her hand on my arm.

A blanket of mist drops, shrouding the lake in ribbons of fog, which chase each other like a posse of ghosts in an elaborate game of twister.

A whisper of wind clears the air.

Sitting cross-legged in the middle of the water are a row of four smoke humans. Eyes, nose, mouth, all fading in and out of existence. They look directly at me and hum, shifting up through the vocal ranges, bass, baritone, tenor, hitting soprano, throwing their hands skywards, their black eyes staring expectantly towards the heavens.

I look at the woman.

'Lost souls waiting for a new life,' she says.

'What are they doing?' I say.

'Calling to God. Maybe one day He'll hear them.'

We walk for what seems like hours through a fig orchard, the woman leading the way, easing stray branches aside with a shepherd's crook and whistling something tuneless.

I keep my eyes fixed on the floor, weaving a careful path through clumps of stinging nettles, conscious of my bare feet. 'How much further?' I say, wiping sweat from my face.

'We've arrived,' she says, stopping and pointing her stick straight ahead.

We stand on a wild grass bank, looking down on a lush lawn, a eucalyptus tree in its centre. 'It's huge,' I say.

'A reunion tree,' she says. 'We need the dust arrangers.'

She claps her hands three times. The dirt at the foot of the tree swirls around and around and around, faster and faster, mashing through the grass, circling, making its way up the trunk.

She claps again.

A prism of white light drops from the tree's canopy.

The dirt stops rotating and floats, higher and higher, disappearing into the eucalyptus.

I look towards the top of the light.

A face, a chipped tooth, a mischievous grin.

I burst into tears.

About the Author

Stephen Anthony Brotherton now lives in Shropshire but grew up in the West Midlands. A social worker for nearly thirty years, he currently works for the NHS and is a member of the Bridgnorth Writers' Group and the Shrewsbury Writers' Lab. His first book, *Fractures, Dreams and Second Chances*, was released by the Book Guild in 2021. *Watching the Wheels* is his first collection of short stories.